by Romulus Linney

NOVELS
Heathen Valley
Slowly, By Thy Hand Unfurled
Jesus Tales

PLAYS
The Sorrows of Frederick
The Love Suicide at Schofield Barracks
Democracy
Holy Ghosts
Old Man Joseph and His Family
Tennessee
Childe Byron
El Hermano
The Captivity of Pixie Shedman
The Death of King Philip
Laughing Stock: Goodbye, Howard; F. M.; Tennessee
Sand Mountain
A Woman Without a Name
Pops

Jesus Tales

A NOVEL BY

Romulus Linney

Foreword by Reynolds Price

1987
NORTH POINT PRESS
San Francisco

Parts of this book have appeared in: *The Greensboro Review*, *St. Andrews Review*, *Shenandoah*, and *The Pushcart Prize V: Best of the Small Presses 1980–81*.

Copyright © 1980 by Romulus Linney
Cover painting by Susan Walp
Printed in the United States of America
Library of Congress Catalogue
Card Number: 80-18280
ISBN: 0-86547-021-9

North Point Press
850 Talbot Avenue
Berkeley, California
94706

for Susan

Contents

Foreword

The canonical gospels of Mark, Matthew, Luke, and John were almost certainly published before the end of the first century, within sixty-five years of Jesus' death. Mark, which is generally considered the earliest, was apparently written in the sixties—only some thirty years after the crucifixion and thus within the lifetimes of a number of first-hand witnesses. Why then (for all their immense power and formal originality) were the four gospels quickly surrounded by a maze of adjacent structures, the works we call New Testament apocrypha? This mass of poems, episodes from Jesus' birth and boyhood, occasionally startling (but more often boring) deeds and speeches from his later history was defined by the end of the second century as neither historically nor theologically reliable. The reasons for the proliferation of apocrypha are numerous:

—The inevitable, partly affectionate, partly stunned mythomania that follows the wake of any extraordinary life.
—The manufacture of historic and doctrinal support for

rival Christian sects (what better defense for your position on chastity or money than a story in which Jesus pronounces in your favor?).

—Most basically perhaps, in compensation for the grave deficiencies *as biography* of the canonical gospels.

It is fashionable now to argue that the canonical gospels were intended as proclamations of a faith, not as demonstrations or proofs. They mean to say that the one eternal God became man in a particular place, lived among other men, suffered the cruelest of deaths in atonement for the sins of all men, then affirmed his divinity and the success of his mission by rising bodily from the dead and appearing to his old colleagues. The argument explains the omission from the gospels of vast areas of Jesus' life and personality (and almost surely his teaching) by claiming that such details were unnecessary to the evangelists' purpose.

Yet an amateur may ask, why (if they were going to ignore so many normal narrative curiosities) did the gospels tell even the bones of a story, a life? Why not confine themselves like St. Paul to assertion through letters and essays? The inevitable suggestion is that they were human enough to see how a proclamation is best and most truly made in a *story*, albeit sparse. Why is their story sparse? The possible answers are again numerous:

—Perhaps Jesus was intentionally secretive.
—Perhaps the evangelists therefore possessed no more facts than they used.
—Perhaps (and this seems to me incredible) the evangelists themselves were secretive, concerned to convey a subliminal message to an elite while deceiving the unchosen.

The second answer seems much the most satisfactory. It is certainly the one which both explains the puzzling biographical omissions and preserves the integrity of the evan-

gelists. Their accounts are not lives—not even in the limited
sense of the great anonymous Old Testament life of King
David and plainly not in the sense of Plutarch or Sueto-
nius—because they did not *know* the life in question. They
were first- or second-hand reporters of an immense explo-
sion; they did not know the formula of the bomb itself. Thus
they tell us tantalizingly little or nothing about the family and
youth of Jesus; the influences on his thought, his adult ap-
pearance, his marital status, his human proclivities.

The immediate successors to these first reporters were the
authors of the apocrypha, and they were not so scrupulous.
But standing at a safer distance from the blast, their responses
were more normal. They proceeded, with instinctive narrative curiosity, to invent a personality for Jesus. Or personalities. Anyone who perseveres through the wastes of Hen-
necke's standard *New Testament Apocrypha* (or M. R.
James's older but more charming *The Apocryphal New
Testament*) will discover fragments of a multitude of men, all
called Jesus—from the scary Superchild of the Protevangel-
ium to the cryptic sex-mage of some of the Gnostic gospels
only recently discovered in Egypt.

In the ensuing centuries the successors to the early apocryphal writers have been legion; and as narrative artists,
they have often been much more satisfying. I need only
mention the medieval mystery plays, such novels as George
Moore's *The Brook Kerith* and Kazantzakis's *The Last
Temptation of Christ*, Rilke's poems on the life of the
Virgin. And a majority of these later apocrypha have been
orthodox in their theology, though D. H. Lawrence's story
"The Man Who Died" is a bizarre modern sequel to the
more absurd Gnostic documents. But with the recent decline
of Christian inspiration in all the arts, the stream of apocrypha has shrunk. Devotional tale-telling (more nearly hagga-
dah than apocrypha) has continued in church circles, but I
can think of only two serious secular attempts in the near

past—A. J. Langguth's peculiar but fascinating *Jesus Christs* and Anthony Burgess's *Man of Nazareth*.

Now Romulus Linney provides a third with his *Jesus Tales*. A good part of his earlier work, fiction and drama, imagines the personalities of baffling historical figures—men such as Frederick the Great and Byron. That personal human curiosity has brought him now to the central enigma of our culture—the private Jesus. He begins in the speculations (or embroidered memories?) of the oldest apocrypha—the marital dilemmas of old Joseph and young Mary—but soon he is very much on his own. With occasional nods toward traditional European folktales of Jesus and the disciples, he explores wonderfully the most lamentable omission of the four gospels—Jesus' capacity for fun, his comic sense. The evangelists do hint dimly that Jesus was prone to jokes—Peter and the tax money, some of the exchanges with scribes and Pharisees, the comic potential of the resurrection appearances themselves—but their Lord is mostly grave. And in two millennia of institutional Christianity, that gravity has often been distorted into primness and murderous indignation. If Romulus Linney had done nothing else here—and clearly he has—he would deserve grateful readers for inventing a whole possible wing in the old house of Jesus' name and nature: a laughing god, approachable and tangible, mining our world with the sly cherry-bombs of his love and care.

Reynolds Price

All this began in the days when the good Lord and his great friend Saint Peter made their tour of the world.

Les Littératures populaires de
toute les nations
Paris 1881

By popular tales we mean stories that are handed down by word of mouth from generation to generation of illiterate people, serving almost exclusively to amuse, and but seldom to instruct.

Italian Popular Tales
Thomas Frederick Crane
Boston 1885

All such stories are absurd.

Irenaeus, Bishop of Lyons
c 120 A.D.

Prologue

How Saint Peter Got Bald

Epilogue

How Saint Peter Got Bald

Saint Peter loved Jesus,
said the Basque Country Spaniard,
but he didn't always understand him.

One time they were traveling here in Spain. They walked up and down the roads, the dust spreading out from their heels, naming towns, founding churches, baptizing babies, and doing good.

Early one morning, they passed a farmer on the road. His wagon had hit something and tipped over on its side. His vegetables, his wheat, his wine kegs, cheese gourds, everything, lay spilled out over the road and into the ditch.

It was a mess.

But this farmer, he was calm about it. He was a big, fat fellow, who just wasn't getting himself upset like his wagon was. No, instead he was down on his knees, in a very relaxed way. His hands were clasped together. His eyes were closed.

He was praying.

"Lord Jesus," he was saying, not very loud. He certainly couldn't see Jesus and Saint Peter coming up behind him, or know that they were there. "This is just what I deserve. I am a careless, miserable sinner. I could have seen that big rock in the middle of the road but I wasn't watching. But I'm not going to feel bad about it. I'm going to be grateful for all the good things that have happened to me. Praise God."

Saint Peter was impressed.

"What a healthy, humble attitude," he said to the Lord. "Let's give him a hand, and get all his goods back in his wagon."

Jesus looked straight ahead.

"Keep walking," he said.

"But Lord," said Saint Peter.

"Hush," said Jesus.

They walked right past this unfortunate man, and right on down the road. Saint Peter kept looking back until Jesus told him stop it.

They didn't get very far until they came upon the same sight all over again. Another wagon was in a ditch. This time a whole side of the wagon was smashed in. There was a big load of hay and wood, thrown every which way.

This farmer was on his knees, too, but he wasn't praying. He was swearing. He had one bony shoulder jammed under one side of his wagon-bed, trying to rock the wagon up out of the ditch. He was sweating and straining and swearing, and he couldn't do it.

This was a tough, stringy fellow. Scars on his face and hands. A long, crooked nose, all squashed and damaged looking. And that swearing.

Saint Peter was dismayed. The man was sending one evil curse after another out upon the innocent world. They didn't even make sense, thought Saint Peter, being about highroads that ate manure, and haywagons that slept with their mothers.

But it put Saint Peter off.

"Don't stop," he whispered to Jesus.

Jesus stopped.

"Lord, we better leave this man alone."

Jesus stood right by him, looking down.

"What are you doing?" said Jesus.

The farmer sat back on his heels, scowling. He wiped sweat out of his eyes.

"The hell you mean, what am I doing? What does it look like?"

"In trouble, eh?"

That farmer got up slowly. Lean and stringy, but big and mean.

"If I am, I don't need you to tell me. Get moving!"

And he cursed Jesus roundly.

Saint Peter didn't believe what he saw.

Jesus socked the farmer. He hauled off and belted him. Knocked him flat.

The Lord Jesus Christ did that.

Saint Peter knew it couldn't happen. If Jesus said it once, he said it a thousand times. Don't hit other people. Just don't.

But here he laid this farmer out cold.

Saint Peter put a hand over his face, and shook his head.

When he looked again, he saw Jesus down on one knee. He was fitting one end of his little walking stick under the wagon bed. Jesus glanced at the knocked out farmer, and chuckled. He stood up, pulling on his little stick.

The wagon rocked up out of the ditch. It rolled out onto the road, and stopped. It stood right side up, axles straight. There wasn't a mark on the side that was smashed. All the wood and hay was back where it had been.

"There," said Jesus.

He walked off down the road.

Saint Peter stared at the wagon, and the sleeping farmer. He ran after Jesus.

Who didn't want to talk about it.

Now, Saint Peter was a good man. But he had to be certain in his mind about every little thing, or he worried. He was brave as a lion, when he knew what the trouble was. When he wasn't sure, he got nervous.

I mean, if someone anywhere near him acted cold, he worried. If they seemed disappointed, he worried. And if he saw somebody laughing, and couldn't figure out why, he always thought it was him.

And he came unstrung, and got uncertain, and started making excuses for himself for no reason.

This is what Jesus enjoyed about Saint Peter. He loved kidding him about that, and never got tired of it.

Take the first time Saint Peter took Jesus fishing. He was sure he knew where the big schools of fish would run in the Sea of Galilee that day. He had Jesus up and into his boat before dawn.

They were first out of the harbor. Saint Peter stood up in his boat and called to the other fishermen.

"Follow me!" he shouted. He was out to show Jesus how professional fishermen operated.

Away they sailed, the other boats following. They sailed way out there to the middle of the Sea of Galilee. They couldn't see anything but water, all around.

Saint Peter slacked his sail. He sniffed the air. He slid one hand quietly into the water. He tasted a finger.

In their boats, gliding silently around them, the other fishermen waited.

Saint Peter pointed about a hundred feet to his left.

"There," he said softly.

The nets went out, easily. They weren't thrown. Jesus watched with interest.

"Why don't we throw the nets?" he whispered.

"Because there are so many fish down there, we don't want to scare them."

It was true. They were there.

"Oh," said Jesus.

He peered down into the water. He tapped the edge of the boat with his walking stick, softly.

More fish than anybody can count dived straight to the bottom of the Sea of Galilee.

The nets were pulled through the water. They were pulled and pulled, and they came up empty.

Not one fish.

Saint Peter sat there dumbfounded. When several throws brought up nothing, his boat was soon surrounded by other boats, full of angry professionals. They called Saint Peter, in no uncertain terms, a damn blockhead. They swore about his wasting half a day for them. They sailed off.

Saint Peter rubbed his head. He went over his calculations. He'd never been that wrong before. He inspected his nets. Not a hole anywhere. He couldn't understand what happened.

Jesus said fishing sure was an interesting profession. That made Saint Peter feel very queer.

Which is just the way he felt, running after Jesus down the road, after Jesus knocked out that mean farmer, and then fixed his wagon.

And didn't want to talk about it.

It had Saint Peter all confused. Finally, he just stopped, in the middle of the road.

"Lord, wait a minute!" he shouted.

Jesus turned around and came back to him.

"Well?"

Saint Peter counted it off on his fingers.

"One farmer in a ditch prays to you. You pass him by. Another farmer in a ditch swears at you. You do to him what you plainly tell every Christian never do to anybody, and then you save his neck by pulling his wagon out of the ditch."

"Well?"

"I don't understand. What was so bad about the first farmer? What was so good about the second farmer? If something was so good about the second farmer, and not about the first farmer, why hit the second farmer before helping him? I can't find the sense in it."

"Try," said Jesus.

It was getting close to noon, and hot. Jesus saw a good shade tree a few yards off. He laid himself down beneath its branches, ate a pear from his pack, and took a nap.

While Saint Peter tried. He figured things this way, and he figured them that. He paced about in circles, drew lines and arrows in the dirt, put one stone over here and another over there and lined them up in different ways, rubbed his head and knocked his fist against his palm. He thought about it from every side, top and bottom.

When Jesus woke, Saint Peter was ready for him.

"Lord, I understand."

"Good," said Jesus. He yawned.

"A decent man's curse is better than a shifty man's prayer."

Jesus seemed impressed.

"That's it. Isn't it?"

Jesus complimented Saint Peter on his powers of deduction. Saint Peter blushed with pride and pleasure.

Jesus yawned again.

A spasm of doubt hit Saint Peter.

"But if the second farmer was so decent, and the first farmer wasn't, why hit the second farmer and not the first farmer?"

Jesus stretched, and shook himself awake.

"Because if the second farmer was too proud to be helped, which is possible, and had to be put to sleep so you could help him, which is reasonable, then why was he worth helping in the first place, being proud? And if the first farmer—"

But Jesus was off down the road again. His step was light and bouncy. He was feeling good about the pleasant afternoon, and wasn't going to say any more about it.

Saint Peter felt queer again.

He ran down the road after Jesus, thinking as he ran. He rubbed his head, and scratched his head, and rubbed his head, and scratched it.

That is how Saint Peter got so bald so young.

Part One

Old Man Joseph and His Family

Old Man Joseph
and His Family

His workshop,
say the Apocryphal Gospels,
was dusty, and there were cobwebs and rust where he couldn't see any more, but he still went there every day. He often forgot what he was making.

Just before she died, his wife told him he had to stop working. He was too feeble. He was going to fall down, break an arm, hip, or his neck, and die in there.

Now she was dead a year, and still Joseph went to his workshop, talking to her out loud, saying he'd be all right.

One day he was binding a double brace he used inside platforms. He didn't mix his glue right. He let it boil too long. He took off the clamp too soon. The slats came unstuck. One hit him on the head. Another slid between his legs. He tripped and fell down, hard.

He got up on his left side, but slipped and fell again. He tried his right side, and the same thing happened. He couldn't get himself off the floor.

He lay there.

"God damned miserable old age," he said.

He heard footsteps. There was a loud knock on his workshop door.

"Come in!" he said.

The door opened. A tall man in a dusty cloak stood looking down at him.

"Are you Joseph the Carpenter?"

"That's right."

"Want me to help you up?"

"No, thanks."

"Suit yourself."

The tall man unrolled a scroll with many names on it.

"I have you down here as a widower. Correct?"

"What's that to you?"

"You'll see. Are you drunk?"

"No. Who are you?"

"I am a Herald of the High Priest of the Temple at Jerusalem. Have you married again?"

Joseph stared up at the Herald.

"Of course I married again. I'm only eighty-nine."

"Widower. How many children?"

"Fourteen. Forty-one grandchildren."

"How many live with you?"

"None. They come and I yell and they go. I don't want them around."

"Then you'll have to go."

"Go where?"

"At noon tomorrow, every unmarried male of the House of David will stand on the Temple steps, before the High Priest."

He picked Joseph up and put him on his feet.

"I was married!" said Joseph.

"You're not now."

He looked around Joseph's shop, at the abandoned work

and the old tools. He saw a crooked stick, leaning against a wall.

"You'll need this," he said, taking it to Joseph. It was warped, bent, chipped, scraped and battered, like its owner, but still in one piece. "Everybody has to bring one."

"One what?"

"Shepherd's rod. Orders."

"I'm not going anywhere!"

The Herald put his arm around Joseph.

"Lift your feet," he said.

At noon the next day, on the Temple steps, their rods in their hands, a hundred unmarried men stood in the hot sun, with Joseph waiting in the middle of them.

The great carved doors of the Temple opened. Priests marched out, in flowing robes. Behind them, eyes flashing, came the High Priest.

Behind him, head bowed, walked a girl.

The High Priest stepped forward and looked out over the sea of young men. He made one swift motion with his right hand. Two Priests brought the girl forward.

She looked fourteen, maybe fifteen years old.

She was crying.

"Behold this woman!" said the High Priest. "Ten years ago, her mother brought her to this Temple, as a pure and sanctified virgin. We took her in. Yesterday, she reached her fifteenth birthday. She is now a woman. She must become a wife and a mother. That is law."

The girl wept.

"Since her mother gave her to us, we have treasured her, fed her, clothed her, and brought her to womanhood. Now she disobeys us. Her time comes, she refuses to marry."

The High Priest held up his arms.

"Men of Judea!" he said. "One of you will become her

husband. You will take her, protect her, cherish her, break her, and make her the woman she must become. Hold up your rods!"

All the young men held their rods up over their heads. They were all thin and straight and strong.

Joseph didn't bother, but the High Priest saw him, and said, "You, too."

So Joseph held up his crooked old dried-out rod. He winked at the girl, and smiled.

The High Priest closed both eyes, threw his head back, and prayed. He prayed and prayed. All the other Priests chanted.

The girl stared at Joseph.

The High Priest stopped praying. The Priests stopped chanting. The High Priest was staring up into the sky.

"Men of Judea!" he said. "Look there!"

Everybody looked up into the sky, where the sun was hot and glaring.

"What's happening?" said Joseph, squinting.

"Men of Judea!" said the High Priest again. "Hold up every rod!"

They all did, and Joseph held his up, too.

"What's up there?" he asked a boy standing next to him.

"A bird," the boy said. "Flying around in circles."

"Watch out," said Joseph. "Temples and birds, watch out."

His arm got tired holding up his rod, so he set one end on the ground.

"What's the bird doing now?"

"Coming down."

"Here?"

"Looks like it."

With a flutter of grey-white wings, a large dove sank

down upon them. It perched on the tip of Joseph's rod.

"What?" said Joseph. "What?"

The dove had tiny black eyes. It looked at Joseph.

Joseph shook his rod.

"Get off there!"

The dove had thin sharp claws. They sank into the wood.

"Shoo! Go on!"

The dove stuck fast to the rod.

"What is your name?" said the High Priest to Joseph.

"Get off!" said Joseph.

"Name!" said the High Priest.

"Joseph the Carpenter!" said Joseph. "Go on! Off!"

"Age?"

"Eighty-nine! Get off!"

The dove stuck tight to the tip of Joseph's rod, staring at him with little black eyes.

The girl stepped forward.

"Joseph," she said.

"What?"

The dove opened its claws. With a single lash of wings, it was gone.

The girl stood above Joseph on the Temple steps, looking down at him.

"If you want me," she said, "take me."

"At my age?"

The girl bit her lip.

"What would I do with you?" said Joseph.

The girl nodded.

"Sorry," said Joseph.

The girl stepped back. She bowed her head again.

"You were the perfect man," she said.

She looked up again, bleakly.

"What are you staring at?" said Joseph.

"Hot boys. Goodbye, Joseph."

Joseph looked at the High Priest. He looked at all the young men, with their rods in their hands.

"Listen," he said. "It's not so bad, getting married. Young men are all right."

The girl began to cry again.

Joseph scowled at the High Priest. "You played some kind of damn trick with a trained bird or something. I know that. What's her name?"

"Mary," said the High Priest.

"Tell her to hush up. She's crying again."

"You tell her."

Joseph leaned on his rod.

"Mary," he said. "Hush. Don't let them see you acting like a child. Just because you got to marry some yokel. What did you expect?"

"I'm not crying," said Mary.

She wept.

It came out before he knew what he was saying.

"I might could use me a housekeeper."

Mary stopped crying. The High Priest smiled. The boys winked at each other.

"For just a little while," said Joseph. "I'll be dead soon."

Mary nodded gravely.

"And I ain't the perfect man for nobody. You'll see that, quick enough. And be on your way."

Mary kept on looking at him gravely.

"You'll keep the house. I keep my shop. You don't go in there at all. Understand? Are you just looking or are you listening to me?"

"I'm listening to you."

"I won't lay a hand on you. As if I could. So we'll have no talk of marriage."

"Yes, we will," said the High Priest.

Joseph scratched his head.

"Well, if she doesn't like boys a year from now, and I am still alive, which ain't very likely either one, then we can marry. How's that? Satisfy the Temple?"

The High Priest nodded.

Some of the young men snickered, and nudged each other, wagging their heads.

Joseph glared at them.

"Satisfy you twits?" he said.

He turned to Mary.

"Satisfy you?"

Mary ran down the steps of the Temple, and held his hand.

"I am a plain country man."

"I'm glad."

"We will live in Nazareth."

"That's fine."

Joseph took a step backward, and looked her over.

"My children see you, they are going to piss green. I beg your pardon. I'm a old man. I swear sometimes."

"Yes, sir."

"Call me Joseph. Swearing bother you?"

"When other men swear, I see darkness," said Mary. "When Joseph swears, I see light."

"What will you say to my children?"

"That I like hard work. I have a good disposition. I will take care of you."

Joseph and Mary walked away, together.

"And the town? They'll make fun of us, Mary."

"I don't care, Joseph."

Without looking back, they left the Temple.

"Sooner or later, you are going to think again about hot boys. It's natural. I won't keep them away from you."

"You won't have to."

"Yes, I will. What do you think you'll do, in a year?"

"Marry Joseph."

"Hush. On my ninetieth birthday?"

"Joseph."

"What?"

"It isn't the end that's important," said Mary. "It's the beginning."

Two years later, Joseph was ninety-one, and married to Mary. He looked thirty years younger. His ear aches were long gone. His balance and appetite were back. He was nimble and spry.

His days came and went smoothly again, as he remembered them from his youth, when he thought they had no end.

His children were astonished. All the bad jokes stopped. They became a welcome sight, the healthy old man, and his young wife, who had made him well.

Good as her word, Mary took care of him. She kept his house neat and clean, gave him hot meals, washed his clothes and cut his hair.

Joseph sat with her through long evenings. He listened carefully to what she told him. About the Temple, and how she had lived there so long. About her mother, who put her there, insisting she was a holy child, marked by God. Joseph said it was all understandable. He'd seen stranger things. She was as fine a young woman as any man could find anywhere. Forget the Temple.

So.

He cleaned up his workshop. His working ways came back to him. He invented a wooden window lattice that could fly open or shut tight at the pull of one cord, and was much admired. He made all kinds of furniture, and every piece was smooth and sturdy. In their places, glistening now, were his double-handed saws, squares, files, mallets, hatchets, awls, his glue-pots, chalk lines and plummets, all looking formidable.

Men came to see him, asking him questions. A contractor hired him to supervise not only the woodwork inside his buildings, but the digging of the foundation hole and the perpendiculars of the stones and the mortar.

Joseph was in demand, not just as a carpenter, but as a builder of long life and experience. He was sent on trips to other towns where he was made much of, and so he found himself back in the rush of life.

One day Joseph was getting ready for another trip, and Mary was trying to tell him something.

"Joseph," said Mary. "I have something to tell you."

Joseph was packing a small leather bag, not paying attention.

"Joseph, I have something to tell you."

"Eight houses. This is going to be some trip."

"Joseph."

He looked at her fondly.

"Marrying you was the best thing that ever happened to me, honey. Now, what is it?"

"I'm pregnant."

Joseph lifted his leather bag by its rope, still smiling.

"What did you say?"

"I'm pregnant."

Joseph put the bag down, and stared at her.

"I'm going to have a baby."

Joseph sat down, suddenly.

"I think it's about three months now."

Joseph looked at his bag, at the floor, at the ceiling, and then back at her.

"Joseph. Say something."

"My virgin Mary? Three months gone?"

"That's right," she said.

Joseph thought for a moment.

"Take me," he said. "You are the perfect man."

"Joseph."

"I like hard work. I have a good disposition."

"Stop that."

"I'll take good care of you."

"Joseph, listen to me."

"Didn't I give you a year? Tell you to find your hot boy when you need him. Didn't I tell you that?"

"There isn't any him."

"What?"

"That's what I am trying to tell you."

Joseph closed his eyes. His left ear began to ache again. There was a tremor in his right hand.

"I am still a virgin," said Mary.

Joseph took a deep breath.

"Honey, I am ninety-one years old. I just don't want to hear talk like that."

"But it's the truth, Joseph."

Joseph sat up straight in the chair. There was a cramp in his side. There was a buzzing at the base of his skull.

"Don't you want to know how it happened?"

His tongue was sticking to the roof of his palate. His mouth tasted like damp clay. His eyes began to ache.

"All right," he said, wearily.

Mary sat down across from him, and spoke slowly, and carefully.

"You were on a trip. I went to the well. A young man was standing there. He was singing a song. It was about rosy lips and being in love. He was singing it to himself, and he had smouldering dark eyes, Joseph, but the brightest yellow hair. He didn't look like anybody I'd ever seen before. He kept staring at me. He made me very nervous."

"Nervous," said Joseph.

"I drew the water and came straight home. I couldn't stop

thinking about that young man. And for some reason I got sleepy. More sleepy than I have ever been in all my life. So I went to my room, and lay down, and took a nap."

"Nap," said Joseph.

"In my sleep, I heard the song again. I dreamed that it woke me up. I dreamed I went to the window and looked out and saw that young man, with the dark eyes and the yellow hair. He was standing outside the house, singing."

"Singing."

"He opened my window and climbed into my room, and with him came fresh air and sunlight. It was dazzling. He took me back to my bed. I lay down again. He knelt beside the bed. He told me something wonderful was going to happen to me."

"I bet he did."

"Then I saw the wings he had on his back. They suddenly moved, and stretched. They were dark green and copper colored, and they went up and down slowly, like big fans. He bent over me. He whispered in my ear. He said I was going to have a holy baby. That's what he said. Then he blew gently into my ear. I felt wonderful. He sat by me, singing his song about rosy lips, and being in love. He melted into sunshine and fresh air. I dreamed a star fell into my mouth, and then I woke up. And I was in my bed, in the afternoon again."

Joseph nodded.

"Well, Joseph?"

"Well, what?"

"You are my wise husband. What does it mean?"

"There's only one thing it can mean."

"What's that?"

"You get pregnant through your ear."

Mary jumped up.

"You're laughing at me!"

"What else can I do?"

She sat down again, biting her lip.

"Look here," said Joseph. "That is some story. You have told it to me, and we will leave it at that. I am trying to keep calm. But you had better tell me another story."

Mary shook her head.

"I got to hear something that makes sense."

They stared at each other.

Then they heard a man singing. He was going by the house, singing a song about rosy lips.

Joseph hopped to the window and looked out.

"That's him!" said Joseph.

"Who?"

"Your goddamned angel, that's who!"

Joseph's rod was leaning against the wall. He grabbed it.

"What are you going to do?"

"I'm going to bust up some copper-colored wings, that's what I'm going to do!"

He opened the door and rushed out. Mary didn't know what to do. Joseph meant her to stay in the house. He'd slammed the door.

She went to the window.

Joseph was out there waving his rod. A man was backing away from him.

"You're crazy!"

"Stay where you are!"

"Get away from me!"

"Come on and fight!"

The man ran away. A hundred feet off, he stopped and turned back.

"You ought to be locked up!" he yelled.

Then he was gone.

Joseph leaned on his rod. He couldn't get his breath.

"Scoundrel," he gasped.

He stood there for awhile, getting his breath. Then he went slowly back into his house.

"Did you see the coward run away?" he said to Mary. "Dark eyes and yellow hair. Love songs. Hanging around my house."

"Joseph," said Mary. "The man at the well I saw was one person. What I dreamed about was another person. This was somebody else entirely. You still don't understand."

"Oh, yes I do."

He sank down into a chair, exhausted.

She waited to see what he would do.

"I can divorce you," said Joseph.

"Do I have to go back to the Temple?"

"And have your baby there?"

"Oh."

"Not likely."

"No."

"Go where you please. Try somebody else."

"There won't be anybody else. There wasn't even anybody else this time."

"Don't say that again."

"God can do anything."

"But He don't. He made the rules. He sticks to them. Virgins don't have babies."

Joseph sighed. He was sinking fast. All his aches and pains were coming back. He was aging a year a minute.

He'd been alive again. He didn't want to die now.

He watched her. She was upset but ready to face whatever came next.

Suppose he did figure out what actually happened? Then, no matter how it happened, or who that angel really was, she'd have to leave.

And he would die.

So.

He leaned back in his chair.

"When my children hear you are pregnant, they will piss green."

"Why, Joseph?"

"They'll know I'm not the father."

"Will they?"

He thought about that.

Outside the house, clouds passed away from the sun. Light came in the window. It fell on his leather bag, packed and ready to go.

Busy men were waiting to make the trip with him. Consult with him. Listen to him.

An old man betrayed by a young wife, that was one thing. But Joseph betrayed by Mary? Who would believe it? He had trouble believing it himself.

If he accused Mary of that, his children would make him wish he'd never been born.

On the other hand, a baby at his age?

Who would say what?

So.

He noticed that his earache was gone. He held out his right hand, and it was steady. He could breathe easily again.

"We better not do anything sudden," he said. "I got to go on my trip."

"Do you want me here when you get back?"

"That'll be all right."

"Joseph. I have to ask this."

"No, you don't. What can I say? The baby ain't mine, it's a green-winged angel's?"

"Joseph, will you say it's yours?"

"I won't say it ain't."

He picked up his leather bag, and got his rod.

Mary went to the door and opened it for him. The men with their wagons had gathered outside, and were waiting for him.

"Be careful," said Mary.

Joseph eyed her narrowly.

"You, too," said Joseph.

Into a courtyard, hand in hand, walked a bride and a groom, just married. They were very young and handsome and healthy and miserable. Behind them walked an old woman with a black shawl over her head. She was miserable, too.

"Is it open?" said the bride's father.

"It is not," said the old woman. "They locked it."

"Give her the key," said the groom's father.

"Don't do it," said the bride.

The road to Nazareth went right past the courtyard gate. Mary, holding her baby, peeked in.

"Oh, Joseph, look," said Mary. "A wedding."

She smiled at the bride and groom.

"I hope you'll be as happy as we are," she said.

The groom hung his head. The bride turned away.

"What's the matter?" said Mary. "Did I say something wrong?"

"You must have," said Joseph. "Come on."

The parents of the bride and groom saw the baby in Mary's arms, and how old Joseph was. This was an unusual family.

"Just a minute," said the bride's father.

"You are a man of experience," said the groom's mother.

"And wisdom," said the bride's father.

"Stop with us awhile," said the bride's mother. "Rest yourselves."

"And let us talk to you," said the groom's father.

Mary and Joseph went into the courtyard.

"We have a tradition here," said the groom's father. He pointed to the old woman. "She must inspect the wedding bed the day after the wedding night."

Joseph nodded. "No blood?" he said.

"The bride and groom," said the old woman, "have locked the door. They won't let me in."

Servants brought Mary a chair, and an umbrella to keep the sun off the baby. They brought soap, towels, a basin, cups of lime juice, and a jug of cold spring water.

Joseph watched until Mary was settled. Then he spoke sternly.

"Young married people!" said Joseph. "The least you can do is use chicken blood. That's what folks do where I come from."

"No, no!" said the bride's father. "It's too important! Negotiations depend on this!"

"Land grants, mergers, other weddings," said the groom's father.

"I'm talking to them," said Joseph. "Speak up, young married people. I won't fault either of you for what you say."

"You can talk to him," said Mary. "Don't be afraid."

The bride and the groom looked at each other, and nodded. They stepped aside with Joseph and whispered to him.

"We got into bed," said the bride.

"After we said our prayers," said the groom.

"We put our arms around each other," said the bride.

"To begin our married life," said the groom.

"And nothing happened?" said Joseph.

"We did our best," said the bride.

"Nothing happened," said the groom.

"Fancy wedding," said Joseph. "There it is."

Mary spoke to the bride. "Could you hold the baby?" she said.

"Of course," said the bride. She took the baby from Mary, and held it in her arms while Mary washed its face.

The groom stood beside her. He touched the baby's palm with his finger. The baby's little fist closed over it.

"He's strong," said Mary. "Like his father."

The bride leaned against the groom, and watched the baby hold the groom's finger.

"Can't you try again?" said Joseph. "Start the whole thing over?"

"Impossible," said the bride's father.

"The contracts are very specific," said the groom's father. "All negotiations are cancelled today, unless those sheets get inspected."

"Well," said Joseph. "That's too bad."

The groom smiled at the bride. The baby let go of his finger. The bride gave the baby back to Mary.

"We should call it off," said the groom's mother. "Everybody makes mistakes."

The groom kissed the bride. The bride kissed the groom.

"If children can't do it, we shouldn't force them," said the bride's father.

"Call it off," said the bride's mother.

They turned to tell the bride and groom. Neither were there.

"They left," said Mary.

The parents of the bride and groom shrugged their shoulders, and looked at each other sadly. They asked Mary and Joseph who they were and where they were from and how old the baby was.

"We live in Nazareth," said Mary. "The baby was born in Bethlehem, just a few days ago. In a farmer's cave, because we couldn't find a room."

"You mean, with all the livestock?" said the bride's mother.

"That's right," said Mary. "Just as he was born, three old men appeared."

"Three drunks," said Joseph.

"And three shepherds," said Mary.

"They got drunk, too," said Joseph.

"The three old men were magicians," said Mary. "They had charts and glass globes they swung about on strings. A star told the shepherds where to find us."

"Evidently an unusual birth," said the groom's father, politely.

"No, indeed," said Joseph, quickly. "It's not a baby's fault what kind of crazy people are running around the night it's born."

Mary smiled.

"The farmer did get us a midwife," she said. "But I felt no labor pains."

"What was that?" said the groom's mother.

"Discomfort," said Joseph. "But no hard pains. It happens sometimes."

"That night," said Mary, "the midwife washed the baby, and took the water home. The next day she said she'd used it on a grandchild with boils, and they all disappeared."

"She was crazy too," said Joseph.

"That's what she said," said Mary.

"It was a long night," said Joseph. "But the baby's all right."

He looked at Mary.

"And he's going to stay that way."

"Of course," said Mary.

"He is just a plain, run-of-the-mill little boy, and I mean to keep him that way."

Joseph wouldn't let Mary say any more about the baby's birth. He thanked the parents of the bride and groom and got Mary ready to leave.

The bride and the groom came walking back into the courtyard, arms around each other.

Behind them came the old woman.

"Blood!" she said. "Blood!"

"Let's go, Mary," said Joseph.

The parents blocked their way, and wouldn't let them pass.

"The baby was holding the groom's finger," said one.

"The bride was holding the baby," said another.

"It's a holy child!" they all agreed.

"God damn it!" said Joseph.

"Don't scare the baby," said Mary.

"God damn it!" said Joseph.

It was a year later. Joseph came pulling a wagon he made for Jesus into his workshop. It was a playpen on wheels. He could pull it from his workshop, and have the baby with him while he worked. It gave Mary a little time to herself.

The pen had solid wood siding, which made it very safe. There was a metal brace that took the shaft of an umbrella, which could open up outside to keep the sun off the baby.

Joseph maneuvered the pen so it fit against one wall of his workshop. He went to his bench, sat on his stool, and went to work.

The baby, left alone, made a fuss.

"Hush up, Jesus," said Joseph. "Stop your crying. Your birthday is almost over. You're a whole year old today, so settle down. Play with your blocks. Daddy's got to work."

He sharpened a carving tool. Then he took a hatchet and split a piece of cedar. He held it up and then, with his chisel and a mallet, he began to knock it into shape.

He heard little knocking sounds in the pen.

Jesus was banging his wooden blocks.

"That's it," said Joseph.

With a file he began to sand the edges of the cedar.

"Yes, sir. Things are going along all right now. Your mother is beginning to see what I mean when I say you're no different from anybody else."

He stopped filing. He used his mallet again.

"Your mother," he said.

He used his file again.

"Truth is, your mother's not that much older than you are, not to me. You two are going to be close. I can see that."

He heard filing noises inside the playpen. He looked in. Jesus was scraping a small comb against a block of wood.

He went back to his bench.

"It's up to me to teach you, Jesus. You're nothing special. Get that through your head. It would be the worst thing I could do to you, son, to tell you you are. Puff you up like a fool. Let you believe everything your Momma tells you is the truth. Send you out in life thinking you are God knows what. That's what happens to Momma's boys, Jesus. They're just one little grain of sand, like what's coming off this wood, but they think they hung the moon. Truth is, there's nothing in their minds but Momma. They end up good for nothing, in trouble all the time, and accomplish not one thing unless it's get theirselves hung someplace."

He turned his file on its side and cut into the wood. It made a rasping noise.

A rasping noise came from the play pen. He got off his stool again and looked back into the pen. Jesus was scraping a brush against the side of the pen.

He went back to work.

"Jesus," he said, "I've watched Momma's boys all my life. They play hell with everything. You take my great grandson, Laban. He has got to be the second horse in every stable. Other men's women. One after another. One time I swear he told me it was best when he couldn't hardly see their faces. Faceless women. Now, I ask you, Jesus. You know what that is? Just a grown man trying to become a baby. I ain't letting that happen to you! No sir! Never mind worse, end up playing with other men, like my grandson, Gomer. Hell, no!"

He was almost shouting.

He stopped his work and wiped his brow with a rag. He looked over his shoulder at the pen.

"How you doing in there?"

A little shout came from the play pen.

He dipped the block of wood into a bucket, looked at it closely while the solution of oil and grease sank in.

"Or my son, Michmas. He thinks he has got to run the world his way or it will just fall down."

Joseph rubbed the wood with the heel of his hand. He stood up, got a bottle of a greenish colored oil, poured some of that into the bucket, and dipped the wood in again, and held it there.

"He was my firstborn. Now look at him. A cruel old man."

Joseph pulled the cedar out, dried it off with one rag and began to polish it with another.

"Bloated in mind and body. Nothing nowhere that ain't his. A god damned hog. I ain't letting that happen to you, neither! No, sir!"

He hopped off his stool, excited. He rubbed the wood. He sniffed it, made a face, then soaked it in oil and grease again.

"Momma's boys," said Joseph. "All three."

He poured rainwater from a tin bucket into a smaller wooden bucket. He put the cedarwood into the smaller bucket and swished it around.

"I love your mother," said Joseph. "But you ain't a toy for her to play with. You are something else."

He took the wood out of the water. With dabs he worked fingertips of oil into its side.

"What else? You are my father, and his. You are the straight plumb-line, and the honest building. I didn't get this old, son, for nothing. I know what's in, by God, and I know what's out. I know squared off beams, set so flush an ant can't get between. I know fine wooded floors, polished so the dust rests on it easy to clean. I know the fireplace drawing strong, and the home that's built to last."

He blew on the wood. He took his cutting tool, and he quickly began to etch in small half circles, one above the other, on both sides.

"I'll show it to you, my boy. You'll come climbing out of that play pen soon enough. I'll take you to town. You'll see men up and doing, baking the bread, opening the stores, making the fires, riding horses, banging hammers and tongs, and in the frosty morning, coming to town for work."

He took a long nail and knocked a hole in each side of the block of wood, toward the front.

"I didn't think I wanted to see it again. But now you're here. I'll show it all to you, just like I never seen it neither. I love you, Jesus. You're my boy. I'll set you straight in this life. Yes, by God. I will."

With a thin sliver of wood, he laid a speck of glue in each nail hole. With a pair of tweezers he set in each hole a flake of silvery mica.

"There now. You're still just a damn baby. Here."

He took the block of wood to the pen.

"Little fishy. See? Oiled it, so it feels like a fish. Made it from cedar, so it has stripes. See?"

He moved it about.

"What fishes do, Jesus, is swim. Wiggle, wiggle. Like that."

He gave the fish to Jesus.

"There, son. Happy birthday."

He stepped back, smiling. He was very happy. He closed his eyes, stretched and yawned.

As he opened his eyes again, a live fish flew out of the pen. He grabbed it.

"Huh?"

He tried to hold on to it. He couldn't.

"What?"

The fish flipped and flopped in his hands. He managed to get it to his workbench. He plunged it into the bucket of rainwater.

He turned around.

"Jesus?"

He went to the pen and looked in.

"Where's that wooden fish?"

Jesus gave him a quiet smile.

Joseph hopped back to his workbench. He plunged his hand into the water bucket.

He pulled out a wooden fish.

"Wait a minute," he said.

He went to the door, and opened it.

"Mary!" he called. "Who's playing tricks on me!"

He stormed out, toy in hand.

Jesus played with his blocks.

It was four years later.

"Goats?" said Joseph.

"Goats," said Mary.

She bit her lip.

"Come on, Mary. God damn it."

"Nobody wants Jesus to play with the other children."

"How long has this been going on?"

"A month. Since the children all got sick, with the eye infection. And Jesus didn't. Somebody said Jesus did it."

"Infected the other children?"

"Yes. Got mad, and gave them the eye plague."

"God damn magic baby. I thought I had that all done with. Here it is again."

"Yes. I'm sorry."

"What about the goats?"

"Yesterday Jesus went out to play with his friends. Their mothers shut them up in one house, and stood at the front door. They told Jesus the children couldn't come out. Jesus went around to the back of the house, and got in. He told the children to sneak out the back and hide, and they did."

Mary took a deep breath.

"There was a goat pen behind the house. Jesus fed the goats some sugar, and then herded them through the back door. He ran around to the front door again and called out the names of the children."

"He did what?"

"He stood there calling out *Come on, Ezra! Jump, Esther! Hop, Ruth!* and those goats came bursting out of the front door, and ran off after Jesus. The women thought Jesus had turned their children into goats."

Joseph turned away, laughing.

"It's silly," said Mary.

Joseph turned back, frowning.

"Don't tell me. I said so five years ago."

"Yes, Joseph."

"God damn it, Mary."

"Yes, Joseph."

It was four years later.

"Where is Jesus?" said the Schoolmaster.

"We don't know," said Mary.

"Speak up," said Joseph.

Joseph's legs were shakier now, and his ears were failing him. He used two sticks for canes, and thrust himself forward to hear.

"Your boy is in trouble," said the Schoolmaster.

"What has he done now?" said Mary.

"My children were all in their places," said the Schoolmaster. "I said, *Say after me, Alpha.* And they all said, *Alpha.*"

"Jesus, too?" said Mary.

"Jesus, too. Then I said, *Say after me, Beta.* And Jesus said, *Tell us what Alpha means, and then we'll say Beta.*"

"Oh," said Mary.

"He upset everyone. I said, *Students, Alpha is the beginning. The Void. Before anyone knows what anything was. The study of scripture is the jump, you see, from the Void to the Now.* And Jesus said, *Well, this is exciting.* I pretended I didn't hear him. *A leap demands Faith, otherwise you will perish in doubt. Have faith, first in me, and you will understand, deep within you, both the Now and Alpha, the Void.* And Jesus said, *I think I understand the Void already,* and the children laughed."

"Oh, dear," said Mary.

"Jesus challenged me in front of my class. *I don't think you know anything,* he said, *never mind what the beginning was. You call it the Void. Is that what we all came from?* And I said, simply, *Yes,* and Jesus said, *God is the Void?* and I said, *Of course not. God is older than the Void, which is only a small part of God.* And Jesus said, *Well, what part of God is it we all come from, then?* And I said, *From the goodness of God, naturally,* and Jesus said, *Which is inside God like the Void?*"

Mary tried to follow the Schoolteacher.

"I lost my temper. *Jesus!* I said, *There is one great Idea that holds everything together. All your study prepares you to comprehend it.* And Jesus said, *I am only a little boy, but let me try,* and I said to him, *There is one God and that one God is good.* And Jesus didn't answer me."

"I'm glad," said Mary.

"For a few minutes. Then, when I had gone on and was in the middle of something else, Jesus said, *Wait a minute, people used to believe there were lots of Gods, true?* And I said, *In their ignorance, some still do.* And Jesus said, *Rain was God. Sun was God. Wheat was God. Love was God. Death was God. Money was God. They were all separate. So if one God was mad at you, it didn't have anything to do with another God. What the rain God did to you had nothing to do with what the love God did to you. If the war God was mad at you, that didn't mean your wheat wouldn't grow, or that the sun God would hold it against you when the money God took away all your money.* And of course, I saw then where he was leading me."

"You did?" said Mary.

"I said, *You want to know how many old Gods, who could be so terrible, can now exist in one good God. Am I right?* Jesus said, *For the first time this morning.* And I said, *The old Gods, separate, held only separate powers. God, until he was recognized as one God, was not all powerful. When he became one God he became all powerful.* And Jesus said, *What does that have to do with it?* and I said, *Since we now know God to be all powerful, we understand him better.* Jesus said, *We do?* I said, *Of course. We see now that God can be all good even when he may seem to be partly evil.* And Jesus said, *Or all evil even when he may seem partly good?* I saw it was no use. I said, *Do not mock the prophets, child.* And Jesus said, *Wasn't it the prophets who said God was a jealous God and a loving God and a God of happiness and revenge all at the same time, just exactly like the old gods, with only one difference, now that he's just one God if you do anything wrong anywhere in your life he can get you for it?* And I said, *Exactly. That is what makes God God.* And Jesus said, *No, it doesn't. That only makes God like my father. That is the worst idea I ever heard. You are a god damned fool.* And he walked out of the classroom."

"School," said Joseph. "I never understood it, either."

"I will speak to Jesus," said Mary. "He will apologize."

"Do I have your word for that?"

"You do."

It was two years later. The women were furious.

"My son was making a clay sparrow," said the first. "Jesus grabbed it. He blew on it and threw it into the air, and it flew away!"

"My little girl was making a clay snake," said the second. "Jesus grabbed it and threw it into the river. A snake as big as your arm came out of the river onto the bank, went after my little girl, and when Jesus told it to, it exploded!"

"All this," said Joseph. "All this again."

"One boy was making a clay lion," said the third. "Another a clay tiger. Another a clay hippo. Jesus said if the children wouldn't do what he told them, he would bring the animals to life and the lion and the tiger would eat them and the hippo would sit on them."

"What did he want them to do?" said Mary.

"Crown him King!" said the first woman.

"We caught him at it!" said the second.

"At what?" said Joseph.

"Sitting our children at his feet, in a circle," said the first woman. "Taking flowers from them, and putting them in his hair!"

"Telling them crazy stories," said the second. "About far off places he would take them to."

"Where they would go and live without their mothers and fathers!" said the third.

"We ran him off!"

"He's a menace!"

"He's a Child Terror!"

"We won't have our children threatened!"

"Leave Nazareth!"

"Get out of town!"

It was two years later.

Joseph and Mary were looking at a beautiful piece of cloth. It was striped in bright and vivid colors that seemed to change as the cloth moved.

"He came to my store," said the Cloth Dyer. "He wanted to work for me. He wanted to know all about dyes. If it was true they came from oak-tree bugs and fruit rinds. I showed him a purple I get from shell fish."

"Woman's work," said Joseph.

"I showed him how I add soap, just a little, to make crimson stick faster to wool. He asked me questions. I let him stretch a piece of undyed wool, and left him alone. After three hours, he was still there. He said it was no good just staining it. He wanted to make fabric and color one thing forever. He said if a piece of cloth was pure white, if the strands of hair could open themselves, then the dye should soak every part of it, and stay there forever. Not as a stain that would fade or come out someday, but as a part of the thing itself, like blood. Then he began to cry."

Joseph tapped his canes impatiently, one against the other.

"What kind of talk is that?" he said.

"But he did it!" said the Cloth Dyer. "He dyed that piece of cloth right there. Then he ran off and wouldn't tell me how he did it!"

"It's beautiful," said Mary.

"Keep it," said the Cloth Dyer. "If he ever tells you how he did it, let me know."

It was that same night. Jesus lay in bed. His blanket was pulled up almost over his head. Over the foot of his bed was draped the cloth he had dyed.

Mary came into his room, and sat in a chair by his bed.

"I should have stopped him," said Mary. "A long time ago. When he tried to make you a man too soon. I didn't know how."

She took a deep breath.

"I was a child myself," she said.

She looked at the floor.

"He meant well. He still does. He's old. He's clumsy. He thinks he knows everything. But it is my fault."

She took another deep breath.

"He never liked it when I took my pleasure in you. He told me we shouldn't be that cozy. It wasn't right."

She frowned.

"I was too good about it. I didn't tell him he was wrong when I should have. He is wrong. You are not a man yet. You need me."

She closed her eyes.

"He shouldn't be so hard on you. All that work. Dragging logs. Fixing tools. Grease and glue. Getting you down in ditches, in the mud and the dirt and making you sweat, for him. That is no way to treat a little boy."

She stared at the wall.

"My son will never be a ditch-digger. Or a carpenter. Or any man's lackey."

She smiled at her son fondly.

"We don't make too much of ourselves. I have not spoiled you. There is nothing wrong with our love for each other. He is an old man."

She touched her son on the shoulder, gently.

"There is more to life than we have. You will find it."

Joseph came into the room.

Mary stood up. She left the room.

Joseph sat in the chair by the bed.

He took a deep breath.

"I should have stopped her a long time ago," he said. "Your mother kept you a child too long. You think the rest of the world has got to care for you like she does. You will end up crazy."

He rubbed his hands together carefully.

"Some men do nothing. Then wonder what went wrong. They didn't say anything, that's what went wrong. When a man loves his son, he tells him the truth."

He put his hands down in his lap. He spoke softly.

"You have got to straighten out. You ain't the sun and the moon."

He sighed.

"I know it ain't been easy. You have a peculiar momma.

And a strange old daddy. But except for me being old and her young, we're not that unusual. We're just people. You can't make us any better than we are."

He spoke firmly.

"We're dust, Jesus. You, your mother, me. Your friends, all this world. Don't stir it up. I'm an old man and I know."

He was silent for a moment.

"It isn't that I don't remember. I had my dreams. About another world. Mine. But King Joseph had to go to work, son. The world put that to him. So I took up my hammer and my saw and I made what I could as well as I could, and that was enough. More, you hear me, is crazy."

He took a deep breath.

"So get it straight, for I will tell you no lies. You're growing up. To please me, you will have to cross your mother. To please her, you will have to cross me. You think about that. Never mind kingdoms."

He stood up.

"You ain't a baby no more."

Joseph left the room.

Jesus lay in bed, his blanket over him. He could hear his parents arguing in the room next to his.

"What did you say to him?"

"What I had to."

"To go crazy, pleasing you? Working himself to death, pleasing you?"

"You want him home all the time? So you can call him your baby? I won't have it. He's going to stand up by himself!"

"But you make him crawl! You make him think he's a ditch digger!"

"Now, Mary! Shut up!"

"He's my son!"

"Mine, too!"

Jesus threw the blanket aside. He jumped out of bed. He put on his clothes. He grabbed the piece of striped cloth. He ran out of the house.

"Jesus!" said Mary. "Where are you going?"

"Jesus!" said Joseph. "Come back here!"

It is late that evening.

Jesus runs, through the town, past shadows and fire, away from voices and outraged cries, running as fast as he can, getting away.

"I saw him!"

"Where?"

"Going past the market!"

The Cloth Dyer stares at his goods with disbelief. His dyes are spilled onto the floor. Bolts of cloth have been taken from their shelves, thrown open and left in tangles.

He runs out into the street.

Jesus races across the town.

An old woman stands in the midst of broken pottery, amazed.

"He was such a nice boy! He called me Grandmother. I showed him my pots and how I made them and he said he wanted to help me. And tonight he breaks into my shop and smashes all my beautiful pots! The devil!"

Jesus runs.

"He's gone past the East Gate!"

"We'll catch him now!"

"What's that?"

"More smoke!"

"It's at the Tile Factory!"

"Fire!"

Blocked at one gate, Jesus turns running back again through the town, dodging the confusion and the angry bodies, leaping behind the buildings, sprinting through alleys.

"Get away from there!"

"You can't do anything now!"

"Look out!"

"The roof's coming down!"

Jesus has one friend only tonight. His name is Zeno, and he is thirteen years old, the same age as Jesus. Standing by the fire at the Factory, he sees a familiar shadow passing. He runs after it.

"That damn boy," says a foreman. "He came here a week ago. He wanted a man's job. I let him run a few errands. Day over, he wanted a day's pay. We laughed at him. Now he's burned down the factory!"

Zeno chasing him, Jesus runs.

"Where is he now?"

"Try the West Gate!"

"Come on!"

A hundred yards from the West Gate, Zeno catches up with Jesus.

"Hey! It's me! Zeno!"

Jesus looks behind him, and slows down. They trot together toward the gate, breathing hard.

"Everybody's mad at you. They're yelling for you."

Jesus nods.

"Did you smash those pots? Did you start those fires?"

Jesus runs to the gate and begins to pull it open.

"They're saying you're a devil!"

Jesus pulls open the gate. Beyond it lies darkness.

He runs out of the city. Zeno follows him.

It is after midnight.

"There!" shouts the Schoolmaster.

Townspeople follow him toward an old shack, in a gulley half a mile outside the city walls. It is held together by old boards and piled up stones. Outcasts go there, lepers and criminals.

The townspeople hold up their torches. There sits Jesus, on the roof of the shack. Below him, on the ground, lies Zeno.

"There!" cries the Schoolmaster. "I told you they'd be together!"

Zeno's father runs out of the crowd. He kneels beside his son.

The crowd gathers around them, talking.

"Look where Zeno's lying."

"Jesus pushed him."

"Is he dead?"

Mary helps Joseph out of a cart. They move slowly toward the shack, Joseph leaning heavily on his two canes.

"What's happened?" says Joseph.

"Jesus pushed a boy off that roof," says the Schoolmaster. "He tried to kill him."

Zeno's father bends over his son, hand on the boy's chest, ear to his mouth.

"Didn't you, Jesus?" cries the Schoolmaster.

In the torchlight, Jesus looks down at the crowd. He smiles a painful smile, a bravado grin boys know well.

Mary and Joseph reach the shack.

"How's your boy?" says Joseph.

"I can't tell," says Zeno's father. "He's breathing. No blood. But I can't wake him up."

Mary stares at the fallen boy.

"Jesus did that?" she says.

"I think he did," says Zeno's father.

"Did you see him do it?" says Joseph.

"No," says Zeno's father.

"Did *you* see him do it?" says Joseph to the Schoolmaster.

"It's plain enough," says the Schoolmaster.

Joseph faces the crowd.

"Who did?" he says.

Nobody answers him.

Joseph turns and for the first time looks up at Jesus.

Jesus looks down, with his twisted smile.

"Son," says Joseph. "I won't ask you again. Did you harm this boy?"

Now slowly the smile goes away from the face of Jesus, as he looks deliberately and coldly straight at Joseph.

"Go to hell," he says.

"Jesus!" says Mary.

"You too," says Jesus.

In the crowd, the women shout.

"His own mother!"

"Child terror!"

"Killer!"

"Zeno?" says his father. "Zeno?"

"God damn it," says Joseph. "Did you hurt this boy?"

"No!" shouts Jesus. "Hey, Zeno. Wake up."

Zeno opens his eyes.

He sits up, holding his elbow.

"Ow!" he says.

"What happened to you?" says his father.

"I fell off the roof," says Zeno.

"Fell off?" says Mary.

"Nobody pushed you?" says Joseph.

"Why no," says Zeno. "I was with Jesus."

He looks up and sees Jesus on the roof.

"He's still there. Hello, Jesus."

"Hello, Zeno."

"They're going to lie about it," says the Schoolmaster.

The crowd agrees.

"Look at Zeno!"

"He's scared to death!"

"Jesus got him up there and pushed him off!"

"Tell the truth, Zeno!"

"Nobody pushed me," says Zeno. "We heard you coming. We climbed up on the roof. Jesus got mad and you made him madder. He swore and kicked at the roof and tripped. I grabbed him. That's all I remember."

"He's lying."

"He's afraid."

"Zeno," says the Schoolmaster. "What were you doing with each other out here?"

"Come on, Zeno!"

"What does Jesus do to you?"

Zeno turns pale.

He jumps up, breaks away, and runs into the shack.

"Zeno!" cries his father.

Before anyone can stop him, Zeno is back on the roof with Jesus.

He has a rock in one hand.

"Leave us alone!" he says.

The townspeople nod to each other.

"See what he does to them?"

"He bewitches them."

"Zeno," says his father. "Come down, or I'm coming up."

"Keep away from us!" says Zeno, holding his rock.

Jesus stands beside Zeno. He takes the rock from Zeno's hand, and drops it off the roof.

"Go home, Zeno. I don't need you."

"You said you did."

"I don't need anybody."

Jesus pushes Zeno off the roof. Zeno lands on his feet, falls and rolls over, crying out. The crowd backs away, astonished.

Jesus grins, baring his teeth.

"Well?" says Jesus to the crowd, to the Schoolmaster and to Joseph.

"Are you satisfied?"

The crowd roars.

"Get that boy down from there!"

"Give him what he deserves!"

Zeno looks again at Jesus, hurt and puzzled.

"Goodbye, Jesus," he says.

"Goodbye, Zeno," says Jesus. "Sleep tight, in your little bed."

Zeno goes away with his father.

Leaning on his sticks, Joseph speaks in a voice thin and quiet.

"He's mine. For what he's done tonight, I'll pay. Nobody's dead. Go home."

Grumbling, muttering, they go.

When everyone leaves, Mary weeps.

"How could you?" she says.

"Down," says Joseph.

Jesus doesn't move.

"Get down," says Mary.

"Or else," says Joseph.

"Or else what?" says Jesus.

Then, suddenly, he pushes off with his hands, and lands before them. He brushes himself off, insolent and trembling.

"So?" says Jesus.

"What's wrong with you?" says Mary. "Apologize to your father."

"Apologize to your mother," says Joseph.

"Never," says Jesus.

Joseph slaps Jesus in the face, as hard as he can.

Jesus grabs both of Joseph's walking sticks, breaks them over one knee, and throws the pieces back at him. They hit him in the face and chest.

Joseph falls to the ground.

Mary rushes to him and kneels beside him.

"Ah!" says Jesus.

He runs back into the shack, leaving them there.

Mary helps Joseph up. When she gets him into the cart, he

sits stunned, hands holding onto the seat. As they move away, Mary doesn't look back for Jesus.

And they too vanish in the night.

Jesus climbs back on the roof. He picks up the striped cloth he'd brought with him. He drapes it over his shoulders. It is very colorful.

He wraps himself in it against the cold, and sits again on the edge of the roof, and swings his feet, shivering.

"To hell with them," he says.

There he sits, a boy in trouble, bewildered and bitter, throughout the night.

Toward dawn, but while it is still dark, a pale figure appears again before him.

It is his mother.

"Come home," says Mary. "Your father is dying."

It is dawn. Mary and Jesus are home. Mary points to Joseph's workshop.

"Go talk to him," she says. "Tell him you are sorry for what you have done."

The old man is sitting on his bench. He looks tiny, shrunken. He fumbles with a nail, and a block of wood. His hands shake. He puts the nail down and turns the wood over and over.

Jesus steps into the workshop.

Joseph fumbles about until he finds his saw. He tries to saw the block of wood. The saw shimmies and jibbers. It bends, springs loose, and flies out of his shaking hands. It falls to the floor.

Joseph sighs. He bows his head.

Jesus sees it plainly.

His father will die.

He shudders.

Mary comes into the workshop.

"Joseph."

Joseph stares, doglike, at the floor.

"Jesus is here."

There is no answer.

A vein in Joseph's head is big as a cord. From the temple, it crawls up over the skull, into the sparse hair. Cheekbones, eye sockets, and skull leap out at Jesus. Joseph's mouth moves, sucks. He tries to lift his arms.

His eyes glitter, like a rat's.

Jesus is thirteen.

"You ought to go to bed now," he says.

Joseph smiles a ghastly smile.

"Old fool," says Joseph.

"What?" says Jesus.

Joseph looks at the block of wood on his table.

"What was I doing with that thing?" he says.

He breathes very hard. He is angry.

Jesus looks at his mother. "What did he say?"

"Hush," says Mary. "Just listen."

Joseph looks at Jesus.

"Wood, mortar, stone," says Joseph.

His rat's eyes fasten on Jesus.

"You won't last, neither," he says. He falls from his bench to the floor.

"Joseph!" says Mary.

"Father!" says Jesus.

They kneel beside him.

Mary and Jesus carry Joseph to a large wooden chair in the corner of his shop.

"Rest here," says Mary. "Then come to bed."

Joseph bows his head. He plucks at the arms of the chair.

Suddenly, he lifts his head, like an animal drinking, who has heard something.

With a shaking hand, he points to the bare wall across the

room. His lips tremble, and spittle drools from the corners of his mouth.

"I see them," he says.

There is no one else in the room. He is talking to the wall across the workshop.

He draws back in his chair.

"They have come for me," says Joseph.

"Who's come?" says Jesus.

Joseph points again to the bare wall of the workshop.

"Angels of Death have come," says Joseph. "I see Azrael there, with his shining sword. With the drop of gall on its tip that I must drink. Behind him stand his minions, all in black. Oh, God."

Joseph shudders.

"Nobody has come for you, Joseph," says Mary. "You're here safe with us."

"No," says Joseph. "I have to go with them. I'm burning, like wood. The wind is at me. Ashes. I have no legs."

Mary kneels before Joseph.

"Rub his shoulders and his neck," she says to Jesus. "I'll rub his legs."

Jesus rubs Joseph's neck and shoulders. Mary rubs his legs.

"I see Gehenna," says Joseph. "Burning, waiting for me. Angels of Death."

Joseph leans back in the chair.

"Jesus," he says.

"Yes, sir?"

"Did you do this?"

"What?"

"Have you killed me?"

"What?"

"Magic. Holy child."

"Joseph," says Mary. "Oh, Joseph."

"Powers," says Joseph. "Great powers. I did you wrong."

His arms fall to his sides. He stares at Jesus.

"Son," he says.

"Yes, sir?" says Jesus.

"I never meant to harm you."

"I know it."

"Then help me."

"How?"

"Go to the window. Tell me if they are out there or not."

Jesus looks at his mother, bewildered.

"Do what he says."

"You're my son," says Joseph. "Tell me the truth."

He shivers, pushing himself back in his chair, stung by cramps and spasms. His mouth is dark.

"Go ahead," says Mary. "He's bleeding inside."

Jesus goes to the window.

Dawn has come. Clouds heavy and sullen hide the sun. The light outside is harsh and glaring.

There is nothing outside the shack. Azrael does not stand there. Neither do his minions, dressed in black. There is no great shining sword, that will cut Joseph's soul loose from his body. There is no drop of gall on its tip, for him to drink. There is no Gehenna. There are no angels of death.

Nothing.

Hot tears come to the boy's eyes. His hands burn from the blow that struck his father to the ground. His tongue, with which he cursed his mother, aches.

Jesus weeps, a man. He feels it bite into him.

He bows his head. He knows what to do.

He returns to Joseph. He takes one of Joseph's hands in his.

He is only thirteen. He is afraid but he speaks clearly and firmly.

"Yes," says Jesus. "Azrael is there."

"Ah!" says Joseph.

"He has come for you. On the tip of his sword hangs the gall you must drink. He will cut away your soul, to take it with him, and your body he will throw into Gehenna. His face is dark. Behind him, dressed in black, stand all his minions, waiting."

"Just as I said?"

"Just as you said. I will tell you the truth. They have come for you, and you must go with them. But I am your son, your holy child. Magic is mine, and powers that reach beyond the earth. Do you hear me? My love for you knows no bounds. Do you hear me? I tell Azrael to sheath his great sword, and stand aside. I command him, and all his minions, dressed in black, be still. Angels of Death must wait."

"I see powers. Great powers."

"I must speak to my father first. Azrael will wait. His face is dark, but it is peaceful, and kind. His sword is in its sheath."

"Powers," says Joseph. "Great powers."

"The rivers of fire are as water," says Jesus. "The seas of demons will be calm. Nothing burns. Nothing will hurt you. I am here. All is well."

"Holy child," says Joseph.

He closes his eyes. He rests. His cramps and spasms leave him.

Mary and Jesus hold his hands.

He opens his eyes again, but he is blind.

"Mary?"

"Yes?"

"Where's the boy?"

"Here with you."

"What's he doing?"

"Holding your hand."

"Which one?"

"This one," says Jesus. "This one."

"Your right hand, Joseph," says Mary. "That gave him the good with the bad. That hit him in the face. That made him toys. That took him to town, to see the men at work."

Joseph smiles a bloody smile. He nods.

"That's right," he says.

When Joseph died, Jesus wept.

Mary closed Joseph's eyes. She folded his arms, crossed his hands, and combed his hair.

"Old Man Joseph," said Mary. "It isn't the end that is important. It is the beginning."

Part Two

Jesus Tales

I

The Man
Who Became Saint Peter

The man who became Saint Peter,
said the Corsican,
wanted a simple life. He wanted to fish, marry, have children
and live quietly.

When he married Perpetua, they had a baby girl. They
named her Petronella. She was a healthy child, with a good
disposition, but when it came time for her to stand up, she
couldn't. Peter put her on her feet, and she sat down again. It
happened over and over.

There was nothing wrong with her legs. Everyone agreed
on that. But Petronella couldn't walk.

Peter couldn't understand it. His daughter stayed lame,
while other children with the same legs ran and jumped. He
was filled with a great purpose.

He said a sort of jingle to himself, over and over:

> *This is my vow:*
> *She will stand*
> *She will walk*

She will dance,
Somehow!

He tried everything. Physicians, magicians, witches. Spells, incantation. Wooden braces, leg irons. Linaments, mudpacks.

Over and over, he set Petronella on her feet, and backed away. She held out her arms to him, and fell down.

Over and over.

As the years went by, Peter suffered bitterly. He didn't even make a good living fishing, since all he thought about was his daughter.

One night, when Petronella was ten years old, Peter bought a cure from a farmer called the Moon Cure. It was a salve, so thick it looked like grease off an old pot, which is exactly what Perpetua said it really was.

The salve was to be used under a full moon, at midnight. Rubbed in hard, like wax. That's what Peter was faithfully doing when he saw that Petronella was blushing.

"She's growing up," said Perpetua. "You can't do this forever."

Peter blushed, too. He asked Perpetua to finish the job, while he stood waiting.

Perpetua did.

And at midnight, when the moon sailed out from behind dark clouds, washing the three of them, father, mother and daughter in a bright magical light, Peter's blood jumped.

He picked Petronella up and held her in his arms. Then, very carefully, he set her on her feet. He kissed her on the forehead and stepped back away from her.

"Walk," he said, softly.

Petronella took a deep breath. Then she took a step forward.

And fell down.

This time, lying on the ground, she wept.

Perpetua called a halt to it.

"It's hopeless," she said. "We'll have no more of it."

She carried Petronella home. She wouldn't let Peter touch her.

Peter felt terrible. What was wrong with her? Why wasn't there something broken, or crooked, that you could see?

He slept badly that night. He dreamed about huge dark lakes, with great fish swimming in them he could not catch.

The next morning, going out early with his nets over his shoulder, he took no pleasure watching the world come to life, filled with light. His catch was poor. He didn't care. All he could think about was his family, and his misery as a father. What difference did fishing make?

That evening, he sat on the beach with his comrades, mending nets. The boats were pulled into shore, and each man sat gripping his net, stretching it out with his toes, and stitching up rips and tears. Peter wasn't doing that very well, either. What difference did nets make?

The fisherman next to him told everyone a story. Peter didn't listen at first, but then he realized the man was talking about a beggar who was crippled, but who got cured, who picked up his bed, and walked.

Peter's blood jumped.

"Who did it? Who did it?"

The man who did it was named Jesus. He was a young miracle worker.

"Where is he now?"

The fisherman didn't know.

It took Peter a week to track Jesus down. To a little town where Jesus and his friends spent the night. They were on a pilgrimage. No one knew what kind. People called them vagabonds. They didn't know where they had gone.

Peter kept after them.

The next town sat on the edge of a desert. Beyond it there was nothing but rocks and sand. But yes, a man named Jesus had been there. He came the night before, with three friends. He left them to go into the desert.

"By himself?" said Peter. "Which way?"

Jesus had been overheard saying he would travel west, with the sun. Peter set off after him.

It was hard hot going. Peter was a fisherman, used to cool dewy mornings, and water under him when the sun beat down. Here he was struggling through dry sand under a broiling sun.

He wondered about Jesus. What kind of a man would be out in such country by himself, under a cold moon at night and a roasting sun in the daytime?

On the next day he found the Lord.

Jesus was sitting alone, on the sand, surrounded by nothing but rocks. He had nothing with him. He was just sitting there, staring. Peter approached him carefully.

He did not look like a very happy man. He was sitting there staring at nothing, sifting sand through one hand. Peter wondered about a man who was so idle, and sad.

Of course the Lord was there for his own reasons, thinking thoughts not always cheerful, since life is hard on everyone, especially him, with that painful cross waiting for him there at the end.

Peter stepped in front of the Lord.

"Is your name Jesus?" he said.

"That's right," said Jesus.

"Mine is Peter. I understand you perform miracles."

Jesus took a moment, and then didn't answer. He suddenly looked up at the sun, squinting.

"It's hot," said Jesus.

"Of course it's hot," said Peter. "I understand you perform miracles."

"I want something to eat," said Jesus.

"So do I," said Peter. "Did you do something to a cripple, so that he picked up his bed and walked?"

Jesus kept squinting at the sun.

"If you please," said Peter. "I'm talking to you."

"Yes?" said Jesus.

"If you made a cripple stand up and walk, you have got to show me how to do it."

Jesus considered Peter.

"Why?" he said.

"My daughter is a cripple," said Peter.

Jesus nodded. "You love your daughter?" he said.

"More than anything!" said Peter.

"Anything?"

"Of course!"

"How about your wife?"

"Well, she's next," said Peter. "And then my work. I'm a fisherman."

"A fisherman," said Jesus.

"That's right," said Peter.

Jesus smiled.

"See that pile of rocks?"

"Rocks?"

"Right over there. Go get two big ones."

Peter stared at Jesus.

"What for?"

"You'll see."

Peter's heart sank. He was talking to a loony. He walked over to the pile of rocks. Around a half buried boulder lay rocks of all shapes and sizes. Peter picked up two rocks. One weighed about five pounds, and the other was a little pebble.

"Here," he said. He handed the Lord the five pound rock, and kept the pebble.

"Now tell me about that beggar," said Peter.

Jesus wasn't sad any more. He hefted his five pound rock. Peter tossed his pebble up and down in the air.

"What about that beggar?" said Peter.

Jesus broke the five pound rock in two. He started eating it.

Peter's blood jumped. The five pound rock had turned into a loaf of bread.

"That's a loaf of bread," said Peter.

"Have some," said Jesus.

In his hand, Peter's pebble turned into a little loaf of bread. "See?" said Jesus.

Peter stared at Jesus. He looked over at the pile of rocks.

"Wait right here!" he shouted.

Jesus did, eating his bread, enjoying himself.

At the rock pile, Peter grabbed that huge boulder with both hands. He rocked it back and forth until it came loose. He pulled it up onto his shoulders. He staggered back through the sand, with that thing on his back. It bent him almost double.

"Turn it into bread!" he cried. "Quick!"

The Lord Jesus was delighted.

Peter staggered about.

John, James, and Stephen arrived. They came out of the desert carrying straw baskets. They were cheerful, healthy fellows.

"Good afternoon, Lord," said John. "Here's cheese and milk."

"Good afternoon, Lord," said James. "Here's meat and fish."

"Good afternoon, Lord," said Stephen. "Here's strawberries and wine."

"Thank you," said Jesus.

"Help!" cried Peter. He collapsed.

"Give my friend a hand," said Jesus.

John bent over Peter. He put both hands on the boulder. It turned into a big loaf of bread. He tossed it like a big ball to James. James tossed it to Stephen, who set it at the Lord's feet, next to the cheese and milk and meat and fish and strawberries and wine.

"Let's eat," said Jesus.

Peter sat up. He rubbed his eyes. He watched them eat.

He tried to think.

"Isn't he hungry?" said James.

"I guess not," said Stephen.

"Pass the cheese," said John.

Peter was a big strong man. People treated him with respect, and he treated them that way. He wasn't suspicious about every little thing. He was used to being with folks who, when they said a fish was caught, it was, and when they said it wasn't, it wasn't. He didn't know what to make of Jesus and his friends.

Watching them eat, Peter had the strange feeling they were putting something over on him.

When they were finished, they smiled at him.

"Good," said John.

"Especially the bread," said James.

"You should have tried it," said Stephen.

Peter glared at them. He pointed at Jesus.

"Did he make a cripple walk?" he demanded.

"Oh, yes," said Stephen.

"Sometime last week," said John.

"No, before that," said James.

"Whenever," said John.

Peter stood up, two big fists clenched.

"Listen," he said. "I came here to see the man who made a cripple walk. I did it because my little girl is a cripple. If you make fun of me, you are scoundrels, and he's one too!"

"Oh," said John.

"Is he mad?" said James.

"It looks like it," said Stephen.

"Hush," said Jesus, to his Saints. He looked sternly at Peter. "What makes you think I can cure your child?"

"You cured a beggar."

"I helped a man cure himself."

"He was a cripple, You said walk, and he did. That's enough for me."

Jesus considered that.

"All right," he said. "You want me to come to your house, say something, and make your daughter walk?"

"I want you to show *me* how to do it," said Peter.

"Oh-oh," said John.

"Ambition," said James.

"You've tried to cure her yourself?" said Jesus.

"For ten years!" said Peter.

He told Jesus about the Moon Cure, and all the others.

"I'm a desperate man," said Peter.

Jesus put both hands on Peter's broad shoulders.

"Follow me," he said.

Peter's blood jumped. To follow Jesus seemed like the best, the most natural thing in the world. He realized it was exactly what he wanted to do.

But it was crazy.

"I have work to do," he said. "A family to support."

He thought of Petronella, and why he came searching for Jesus in the first place.

"He doesn't understand," said John.

"It is too much for him," said James.

"He isn't very intelligent," said James.

They were getting jealous.

"I am the Lord here," said Jesus. "Hush."

The truth was, Jesus was as taken by Peter as Peter was to be taken with him. It didn't bother Jesus that Peter wasn't the quickest fellow in the world. In fact, he liked that. He liked the way Peter rushed into things, got uncertain, and blushed with doubt. He liked the way Peter thought so hard about what he could never understand, but kept on trying.

In fact, he liked everything about Peter.

The truth was, the Lord saw that Peter was able to make him forget for awhile his sorrows on earth, and be amused like plain fortunate people anywhere. To the Lord, Peter was a sudden laying down of his great burden. He was music starting, people kidding around, blind good will and passing contentment, the things that let people bear their deaths and crosses.

Things Jesus did not have time for during his life on earth.

"Follow me," said Jesus again.

It was obvious that he meant it. It was up to John, James and Stephen to go along with it.

"What can you lose?" said John.

"You can see your family," said James.

"When you want to," said Stephen.

Peter knew this didn't make any sense. How could he leave Perpetua and Petronella, to go off after a miracle worker? It was impossible. He only wanted to be a good husband and father, the kind of man who stayed home.

But his blood was jumping. There was something about Jesus that made him feel young and alive.

And he did see those rocks change into bread.

And then, the way they laughed, and enjoyed themselves.

"I don't know," said Peter, looking at the ground.

When he looked up, they were gone. Jesus, John, James and Stephen were walking away from him, fast, with the long strides of men who are used to hard travel.

He couldn't help himself.

"Wait!" he cried.

That's when he became Saint Peter.

2
Early Marvels

Jesus, Saint Peter and the Holy Apostles,
said the Tuscan,
were on the road from Jerusalem to Galilee, when a man came running to meet them. He was shouting, waving his arms and stirring up a cloud of dust.

He fell on his knees before Jesus.

"Lord!" he said. "Help me!"

"Calm down," said Jesus. "What's the matter?"

"My father! He's dying! He's blue in the face. He's vomiting blood. I've given him all my medicines. They don't help!"

"Your medicines?" said Jesus.

"I'm an Apothecary."

"How old is your father?" asked Jesus.

"Eighty-three, Lord," said the Apothecary.

Jesus looked at his Apostles, who looked back at him. He stared thoughtfully at this wretched Apothecary, who couldn't face the death of his eighty-three year old father.

"You love your father?" said Jesus.

"More than anything else," said the Apothecary. "He's a great man."

Jesus picked a little stick off the road and swished it about.

"Do you have a family?"

"Oh, no," said the Apothecary, quickly. "I live with father."

Jesus made little circles in the air with his stick.

"Can you answer my questions, do what I tell you, and believe in me?"

"Yes, Lord!"

"Do you have a bread, pie and cake oven in your house?"

"A what, Lord?"

"A bread, pie and cake oven. In the kitchen."

"Why, yes."

"Is it big enough to reach from here to there?" said Jesus. He pointed with the stick to his foot and then about six feet away.

"I think so," said the Apothecary.

Jesus nodded.

"To save your father," he said, "get him on the baking sheet. Face up. Fire the oven. Slide your father in, just like a pie, and bake him."

"What, Lord?"

"For three hours."

"Like a pie?" said the Apothecary.

"That's right," said Jesus.

The Apothecary turned and ran.

The next day they were on the road from Galilee to Jerusalem. A man came running to meet them, shouting, waving his arms, and stirring up a cloud of dust.

It was the Apothecary. He threw himself at the feet of Jesus.

"What happened?" said Jesus.

"I did it!" said the Apothecary. "I carried him into the

kitchen. I fired the oven. I rolled him onto the baking sheet. Then I slid him in the oven and slammed it shut."

The Apothecary wiped sweat off his face. He took deep breaths.

"I sat in front of that oven for three hours. It was awful. I heard cracking sounds. My father's bones, burning. Then, after three hours, I heard whistling. Then singing."

"What?" said Saint Peter.

"I pulled out the baking sheet. There lay my father, like a man in bed. He was singing a song about love and youth. He said, "Hello, sonny!" Not one hair burned, on his whole white head."

"Wonderful!" said Saint John.

"Marvelous!" said Saint James.

"Congratulations, Lord!" said Saint Stephen.

They all shook hands with Jesus.

"Wait!" said the Apothecary. "I'm not through!"

They turned around to listen to him.

"My father jumped off the baking sheet. He dressed himself up. I had to chase him all over town. He said the most horrible things. He got drunk with the blacksmith, insulted the Mayor, and made indecent proposals to five women and a ten year old boy. It's impossible!"

Jesus nodded. "I understand," he said.

"Thank you, Lord," said the Apothecary. "But what am I going to do now?"

"Your father will get sick again," said Jesus. "If doctors can't cure him, forget your medicines, and mine, and let him go."

"Go?" said the Apothecary.

Jesus nodded.

"Can I do that?"

Jesus nodded.

"There's nothing wrong with that?"

"No," said Jesus. "You can get married and be a father yourself. There's nothing wrong with that, either."

"Really?" said the Apothecary, stunned. "Just—let—him—"

"Go," said Jesus, very quietly.

The Apothecary thought a minute, then sighed. He seemed much relieved. He walked away, slowly, thinking and nodding his head.

"Hm," said Saint Peter.

The rest of that day and all the next, Saint Peter walked ahead of everyone else. Head down, hands behind his back, he walked along thinking.

On the third day, a man came running to meet Jesus and his Apostles. He was shouting, waving his arms and stirring up a cloud of dust.

"The Lord!" he said. "I have to see the Lord!"

Saint Peter stopped him.

"Calm down," said Saint Peter. "What's the matter?"

"I have to see the Lord!"

"I am the Apostle Peter, beloved of the Lord. You can talk to me. What's wrong?"

"My mother. She's dying! This morning blood came out of her ears. Her eyes crossed horribly. She fell down screaming. Nobody can do anything for her. I want the Lord to save my mother!"

"You love your mother?"

"More than anything! She's the greatest woman who ever lived!"

"What do you do for a living?"

"I'm a butcher."

"Do you have a family?"

"I never married. I take care of mother."

"How old is your mother?"

"Seventy-nine," said the Butcher. "When do I see the Lord?"

"Jesus is busy," said Saint Peter.

He bent over, and picked up a little stick from the road. He swished it about.

"Answer my questions, do what I tell you and believe in me. Do you have a bread, pie and cake oven in your house?"

"A what?"

"A bread, pie and cake oven. In the kitchen."

"Yes."

Saint Peter pointed his stick at his toes and then about six feet away. "Would the baking sheet reach from here to there?"

"I think so," said the Butcher.

Saint Peter nodded.

"To save your mother," he said, "get her on the baking sheet. Fire the oven. Slide her in there, face up, and bake her. For three hours."

"You're crazy," said the Butcher.

"I am the Apostle Peter, beloved of the Lord," said Saint Peter. "If you want to help your mother, it's up to you."

The Butcher ran away.

Saint Peter nodded. That was to be expected. He put his head down, his hands behind his back, and walked along again, thinking hard.

Later that same day, they were coming back down that same road when Saint Peter saw a man running to meet them. He was shouting, waving his arms and stirring up a cloud of dust.

Saint Peter thought it would be the Butcher and it was. Moreover, the Butcher had something shining in his hand.

Silver? Jewels? Rewards?

Then Saint Peter saw what he had in his hand, and the smile dropped right off his face, because it was a meat cleaver. The Butcher went after Saint Peter swinging that cleaver in wicked loops and chops. He chased Saint Peter back to Jesus and the other Apostles.

There was a ruckus. There was nothing for the Holy Apostles to do but jump on the Butcher. They got him down on the ground and they sat on him. He squirmed and kicked like a maniac, trying to get at Saint Peter with his meat cleaver.

Saint Peter hid behind Jesus.

"Let me at him!"

"Why?" said Jesus.

"He told me I could save my mother by baking her in the oven!"

"Did you?"

"I did!" said the Butcher. "When I got home, I saw the end had come. I made the fire. I pulled out the baking sheet, put her on it, slid her in and slammed the grate! My mother, burning up. For three hours. Then I pulled her out."

"What happened?" said Jesus.

"What do you think happened?" said the Butcher. "She was burned to a crisp! Down to a little black thing like a cinder! My mother!"

"I'm sorry," said Saint Peter.

"Ahhh!" screamed the Butcher. He tried again to get at Saint Peter with his meat cleaver.

Jesus bent down and took the meat cleaver away from the Butcher. "Let him up," Jesus said.

The Holy Apostles did. They helped the Butcher brush the dust off himself, and apologized for being rough.

"Let's see what we can do," said Jesus.

"Do?" said the Butcher. "What can you do for a cinder?"

"Show us where you live," said Jesus.

They all went to the Butcher's house. They went into the kitchen. They stood looking bleakly down on the baking sheet. There was a charred black cinder lying in the middle of it.

"My mother," said the Butcher.

"How old was she?" asked Jesus.

"Seventy-nine," said the Butcher.

Jesus thought for a minute. "Put her back in," he said.

"What?"

"Fire the oven. Put her back in. Bake her another hour and a half."

The Holy Apostles helped the Butcher. They got the fire going. With great care, so as not to lose the cinder, they slid the baking sheet back into the oven again.

They slammed the grate. They waited.

But an hour and a half is a long time. Some of the Apostles took a nap. Others played stone toss in the Butcher's courtyard.

Jesus lay down for a nap.

Only the Butcher and Saint Peter stayed glued to the spot, staring at that oven.

An hour and a half later, they came running out of the kitchen to get Jesus and the Apostles.

"She's alive!" yelled the Butcher.

"She's singing in there!" yelled Saint Peter.

Everybody jumped up and ran into the kitchen. They all heard her voice.

"Mother?" said the Butcher.

"Pull her out," said Jesus.

The Apostles took hold of the grate, opened it, and seized the baking sheet. They pulled. The baking sheet slid out into the kitchen.

Up went a whoof of smoke. The figure of a woman sat up, smoke curling off her naked arms and legs.

"*Mother?*" gasped the Butcher.

The woman jumped off the baking sheet. The smoke blew away.

"Darling!" she cried.

She grabbed the Butcher. She hugged him and kissed him.

"Ow!" said Saint John.

"Look at that!" said Saint James.

"What a woman!" said Saint Stephen.

Most of her clothes were burned right off her, and she wasn't a day over twenty years old. She had golden skin you could see plenty of, long black hair that streamed down her back. This was a woman to give any man a jolt. Jesus, Holy Apostle, or anybody.

Never mind a Butcher, who knew she had to be his mother.

He tried to get his breath.

"Mother! Please!"

"Oh, darling!" said his mother. "My beautiful baby boy!"

"Jesus!" cried the Butcher. "Help!"

He ran out of the kitchen.

"Darling!" cried his mother.

She ran after him.

"This is serious," said Saint Peter.

"If it is, it's your fault," said Saint John.

"What?" said Saint Peter.

"You got everything mixed up," said Saint James.

"The age wrong, the time wrong," said Saint Stephen.

"I didn't do anything the Lord didn't do," said Saint Peter.

"What kind of stick did he use?" said Saint John.

"Different wood?" said Saint James.

"Fir instead of oak," said Saint Stephen.

"Or thorn instead of yew," said Saint John.

"It was just a stick, lying in the road!" said Saint Peter.

"Mixed up the questions," said Saint James.

"Left some out," said Saint Stephen.

"I did not!" said Saint Peter.

The Butcher ran back into the kitchen.

"Help!" he said.

His mother ran back into the kitchen.

"I carried you inside me!" she cried. "Nothing can keep us apart!"

"Grab her," said Jesus.

The Holy Apostles did. They got the Butcher's mother down and sat on her.

"She feels good!" said Saint James.

"Don't think about that," said Saint John.

"Lord, help!" cried the Butcher.

"Will you do what I tell you?" said Jesus.

"Anything!" said the Butcher.

"Fire the oven again," said Jesus.

The Butcher started throwing wood into the oven.

"Hold her *down*!" said Saint John.

"I'm trying!" said Saint James.

"Think about clouds!" said Saint Stephen. "Think about snow!"

"Now what?" said the Butcher.

"Get in," said Jesus.

"Me?" said the Butcher.

"You," said Jesus. "Quick."

"Darling!" cried the Butcher's mother. "Angel!"

"I'll do it!" said the Butcher. He jumped onto the baking sheet, and lay down.

Jesus slid the baking sheet back into the oven and slammed the grate.

"My baby!" said the Butcher's mother.

"Let her up," said Jesus.

"How long this time?" said Saint Peter.

Jesus was looking at the floor, counting.

"Eight, nine, ten," counted Jesus.

"What have you done to my baby?" said the Butcher's mother.

"Fourteen, fifteen, sixteen," counted Jesus. "Take her over there."

The Holy Apostles led the Butcher's mother away from the oven.

"Twenty-three, twenty-four, twenty-five," counted Jesus. "Now."

Jesus opened the grate. He pulled on the baking sheet.

There was a little puff of smoke.

On the baking sheet sat a little boy, six or seven years old. He rubbed his eyes and looked around.

"Marvelous!" said Saint John.

"Wonderful!" said Saint James.

"Perfect!" said Saint Stephen.

"Darling!" said the Butcher's mother.

"Mommy!" said the Butcher.

They fell into each other's arms.

"The crucial element," said Saint John, "is the heat."

"I think it's the time," said Saint James.

"It's the wood," said Saint Stephen.

Jesus smiled at the Butcher and his mother.

"Bring your boy up easily," he said to her. "Don't be all over him every minute of the day."

She nodded.

"Honor your mother," Jesus said to the Butcher. "But don't overdo it."

The little boy nodded.

Jesus looked at Saint Peter.

"There," he said.

Saint Peter studied the Lord.

"You are something else," he said.

"That's right," said Jesus. "Follow me."

3
Tale of Tales

The first thing Saint Peter did,
said the Sicilian,
after he became an Apostle of the Lord, was to try and cure
his daughter. He came home, picked Petronella up, and stood
her on her feet.

"Look at me," he said. "Listen to me."

"Yes, Poppa," said Petronella.

"She'll fall," said Perpetua, her mother.

"Not this time," said Saint Peter. He let go of Petronella
suddenly, and stepped away from her.

"In the name of the Lord Jesus!" he said.

"Oh!" said Petronella.

"I, the Apostle Peter—"

"She's standing!" said Perpetua.

"Poppa? Momma?" said Petronella.

"It's a miracle!" said Perpetua.

"Command you to walk!" said Saint Peter. "Walk!"

"Momma?"

"Yes, darling!"

Petronella tried to walk, and as always, she fell.

Saint Peter was very unhappy. So was his wife Perpetua. She took Petronella to bed, telling Saint Peter he could go live with Jesus as far as she was concerned.

Saint Peter went straight off to find Jesus. He was disappointed, angry, and humiliated. What kind of Apostle would he be, if he couldn't even cure his own child?

When he found Jesus, the Lord was in a wonderful mood. His rich uncle, Joseph of Arimathea, was sending a ship all the way to Cornwall in Britain, loaded with cloth goods to be traded for tin and glue. Jesus was going along, and he asked Saint Peter if he wanted to go, too.

When Saint Peter said he wanted some help about his daughter, Jesus said, wait until we get back, and Saint Peter said all right.

They had an exciting ocean voyage, and soon they stood together on the deck of their ship, looking at the isle of Britain.

"Is that it?" said Saint Peter.

"Cornwall, Britain," said Jesus.

"Good looking land," said Saint Peter. "Green. Fertile."

"It's a fine place to live," said Jesus. "Of course—"

And he didn't finish.

"Of course what, Lord?" said Saint Peter.

"There is something you should know about the people who live there."

"What, Lord?"

"All the people who live on that island," said Jesus, "have tails."

Saint Peter stared at Jesus. "Oh, hush," he said. "Tails?"

"That's right," said Jesus.

"Have you ever seen one?" said Saint Peter.

"Certainly," said Jesus.

"What do they look like?"

"They are three or four feet long. Covered with red hair. A lot like the tail of a cow."

"There's the harbor," said Saint Peter. "I see sailors working on the dock. They don't have tails."

"They hide them," said Jesus. "Not because they're ashamed of them. They're proud of them."

"Then why do they hide them?"

"Good manners. Some would be longer than others."

"Oh," said Saint Peter.

"Look when they turn their backs," said Jesus. "See those little humps under their coats?"

Saint Peter looked as hard as he could. He couldn't tell if he saw little humps or not.

"If they never show them, how do you see them?"

"You ask."

When the ship docked, Saint Peter found a little time for himself. He walked around the harbor, inspecting the other ships, and looking closely at the Cornish sailors.

At the far end of the harbor, a big strapping fellow was busy coiling rope. Saint Peter walked around him.

The Cornish sailor looked up from his work. "Good afternoon," he said.

"Hello," said Saint Peter. "Nice day."

"It is that," said the Cornish sailor.

"Working hard?"

"As always. And you?"

"Sight seeing. Let me see your tail."

"I beg your pardon?"

"You don't have to be so modest. I understand. Take down your pants and let me see your tail."

Saint Peter came to with a big knot on his head because the Cornish sailor hit him with his rope. He was feeling it carefully when Jesus came by.

"What's the matter?" said Jesus.

"A sailor nearly killed me," said Saint Peter.

"Why?"

"I don't know. I said hello. He said hello. I asked if I could see his tail, and he hit me with a rope."

"Maybe he didn't understand you."

"I said it clearly."

"Try again," said Jesus, and he went off.

Again? thought Saint Peter. He got to his feet.

Another strapping fellow, with a huge axe on his shoulder, came by. He was a Cornish woodcutter.

"What's the trouble, friend?" he said. "Anything I can do for you?"

Saint Peter took a deep breath. "Show me your tail?" he said.

The Cornish woodcutter hit him with the butt of his axe, and Saint Peter went down again. When he came to, he saw the sailor standing by the woodcutter, looking at him.

"I told you he'd ask you that," said the sailor.

"He's going to get into a lot of trouble," said the woodcutter.

They turned to leave.

"Wait a minute," said Saint Peter. "You don't have tails, do you?"

"What do you think?" said the sailor.

"They aren't three feet long, covered with red hair, a lot like the tail of a cow?"

"Of course not," said the woodcutter. "Who told you that?"

"The Lord Jesus," said Saint Peter.

"Oh," said the sailor. "Jokes."

"And him the Lord," said the woodcutter. "Not hardly fair."

The sailor and the woodcutter looked at each other.

"Let's talk this over," said the sailor.

Later in the day, Jesus was walking on the dock, chuckling to himself.

"Three or four feet long," he said, laughing. "Covered with red hair. A lot like the tail of a cow."

Saint Peter, the sailor and the woodcutter, walked up to say hello. Saint Peter introduced them to Jesus and they shook hands with the Lord. Then Saint Peter thanked them for buying him a drink, and said goodbye.

"Goodbye," said the sailor.

"Have a nice time in Cornwall," said the sailor.

They turned around and walked away. Two thick tails, each covered with red hair, a lot like the tail of a cow, came out of holes in the seat of their pants, and slid along in the dust behind them.

"Wait a minute," said Jesus. "They have tails."

"Just as you said, Lord," said Saint Peter, and he walked off, too.

Jesus thought about this for awhile. Then he went after the two men.

He found the sailor coiling rope.

"Hello, there," said Jesus.

"Good afternoon, Lord."

"Nice day."

"It is that."

"Working hard?"

"As always, Lord. What are you doing?"

"Just looking around. Let me see your tail."

"I beg your pardon, Lord?"

"Nobody's watching. Take down your pants, and let me see your tail."

The sailor whopped the Lord in the head with his rope. Jesus went down and out. The woodcutter appeared, carrying a pot of glue and a brush. Behind him was Saint Peter, carrying something long and thin that was wrapped in paper.

"Maybe we shouldn't do this," said Saint Peter, nervously. "He is the Lord."

"He started it," said the sailor.

"You're right," said Saint Peter. "Go ahead."

A few minutes later, Jesus woke up. He had a knot on his head. He had the feeling he was lying on something. He stood up and reached around behind him. Saint Peter came by.

"I have a tail," said Jesus.

"I see it," said Saint Peter. "Four feet long, covered with red hair, a lot like the tail of a cow. What are you going to do about it?"

"I don't know."

"Keep it a secret?"

"It's four feet long."

"Wrap it around your leg?"

"It's two inches thick."

"You're going to have a hard time preaching," said Saint Peter, "with that thing hanging off you."

Jesus shuddered. "Stop," he said.

"What are Christians going to say when they find out you have a tail?"

"I don't want to think about it."

"Or if you're making a miracle or healing somebody, and it comes sliding out of your pants?"

"Please."

"Not to mention when it comes time to rise up into Heaven. Lord, with that tail—"

"All right!" said Jesus. "Help!"

Saint Peter smiled a great smile. "You are asking *me* for help?" he said.

"Yes!" said Jesus.

"Will you believe in me, do what I tell you, all that?"

"Yes!" said Jesus. "Get this thing off me."

Saint Peter whistled. The sailor and the woodcutter appeared. The sailor carried a flat chopping block, and the woodcutter his huge axe.

"What's all this?" said Jesus.

"He who tells tales, Lord," said the sailor.

"Gets caught by them," said the woodcutter. "You won't feel a thing."

He was right.

"I'll get you for that," said Jesus to Saint Peter when it was over.

"We'll see," said Saint Peter. He laughed and chuckled and felt good about it all the way back across the ocean. Traveling with Jesus, having fun like that, it was living.

It was only when his own country was in sight that he remembered his daughter he couldn't cure, and how completely he had forgotten about her.

4

Eternal Summer

Saint Peter's wife,
said the Hungarian,
was not happy when Saint Peter came home after traveling
with the Lord. She did not enjoy his stories of wonderful
adventures and miraculous cures, not when their own
daughter stayed lame, growing up uglier and more miserable
every day, and Saint Peter unable to cure her. She resented
Saint Peter's great love for the Lord.

"He's a fraud," said Perpetua. "Demons, begone. Dead
men arise."

"He's not, and they did," said Saint Peter. "I saw it
happen."

"You poor fool," said Perpetua. "You thought you saw
him turn snow white on a mountain top and talk to Moses,
too."

"I did," said Saint Peter. "He's a God."

"My foot," said Perpetua. She got very angry.

"You were a good man once," she said. "You knew how to
fish and you liked it. You knew how to take care of your

family, and you liked that, too. Now you don't know anything. God, is he?"

"Yes!"

"I'll tell you about God! Last week twins were born across
the lake. Both boys. God spoke to their father and told him if
they both lived, one would kill him. The father told the
grandmother what God said to him. The grandmother
poured boiling fat down one baby's throat."

"Ugh," said Saint Peter.

"There is a good woman around here, a loyal wife. Last
week, her husband decided she was betraying him. He took
her to court. The Judge offered a goat sacrifice to God, and
because the liver was dark, she was guilty, and they cut off
both her hands."

"Stop," said Saint Peter.

"Yesterday a man with eight children was hung for em-
bezzlement. The money was found today. It was all a bookkeeper's mistake. The bookkeeper is the most pious man
alive, who prays to God morning, noon, and night."

"All right," said Saint Peter.

"All kinds of crazy people like Jesus think they are God,"
said Perpetua. "And plenty of crazy people like you worship
them. One bunch where I grew up did it buck naked. They
painted themselves white, stuck chicken feathers in their rear
ends, sang songs about being angels down from heaven, and
did vile things to each other."

"That's enough!" said Saint Peter.

"No, it is not enough!" said Perpetua. "What about that?
Right over there!"

And she pointed to their daughter Petronella, who was
growing up now, but badly, lame as she was. She had all sorts
of skin problems and stammers. She blushed all the time. She
could never look anybody in the face. She sat around all day,
looking at her useless legs. It was sad to see her, so young,
turning cranky and bitter.

"God made our beautiful daughter," said Perpetua. "And then crippled her. Why? Ask Jesus that!"

Saint Peter blushed. He knew he couldn't. He looked at the floor.

"If your Jesus is a God, why doesn't he do something about evil? Twins choked on fat? Stump-armed wife? Eight little children watching their father hang? Chicken-feathered angels? What kind of a God is that?"

"Please," said Saint Peter.

"Why can't he make something nice happen for a change?" she said again. "If he's God."

"I don't know," Saint Peter admitted.

"I'll tell you why," said Perpetua. "He doesn't want to, if he's God. He wants to keep us all helpless and stupid and cruel and miserable and superstitious and vindictive and crippled and afraid of him. And poor. That's God for you."

"Poor?" said Saint Peter. "What's that got to do with it."

"Everything," said Perpetua. "People have hard, poor lives, and that's why they do these dreadful things. If your Jesus was really a God, he would go out and get some money for poor people who suffer, instead of running around the country playing tricks on idiots like you."

And then she wouldn't talk to him any more.

This upset Saint Peter. He loved his wife, even her fierce temper, but this was a time when he was truly upset by it. The more he thought it over, the more he had to admit there was something in what she said.

He went out at once to find Jesus.

The Lord was taking a nap under a tree. Saint Peter woke him up and told him everything Perpetua had said. He was very excited. The more he talked the worse he felt.

"It doesn't seem to bother you that people are so miserable," he said. "Aren't you going to do anything about it?"

Jesus picked up a little brown stick that was lying by his side. He held it up. Two green and white caterpillars were crawling on it, about the size each of his little finger. Jesus brushed them off, gently, and smiled at them.

"You should care more about human beings than you do," said Saint Peter, firmly. "I want to know why you don't."

Jesus made a little hole in the air with his stick.

"Is my wife right or wrong?" said Saint Peter.

Down the road came a man in rags and tatters, staggering. He was haggard and dazed. His bony ribs stuck out of his chest. He trembled all over. His skin was the color of clay.

When he saw Saint Peter and the Lord, even though he was shaking, he stopped and bowed.

"Good day, Lord," he said. 'Good day, Saint Peter."

"Good day to you," said Saint Peter. "You don't look very well."

"I'm not."

"What's the matter?"

"I don't have enough to eat. Neither does my family. I'm sick all the time. I worry. I bite my fingers until they bleed. My wife stopped talking to me long ago. My children hate me. Dogs bark at me, and cats stare me down. I often think I'm losing my mind."

"But what is causing all this, my friend?" said Saint Peter.

"What do you think?" said the wretched man. "I'm poor. That's what's causing it!"

"A-ha!" said Saint Peter, turning to Jesus. "You see?"

A little housecat appeared from nowhere, and rubbed its back against Saint Peter's leg. He gently pushed it away with the side of his foot.

"Perpetua was right," he said. "Poverty is the bottom of it all. If this man stays poor, he might commit crimes, too. Lord, do something."

"What?" said Jesus.

"I don't know," said Saint Peter.

"Give him money?" said Jesus.

"No," said Saint Peter. "That would help his body but not

his soul. Something else. If you're God, think. Help this poor man!"

"You do it," said Jesus. "In my place."

"What?"

"I'll back you up. Go ahead."

Saint Peter stared at the Lord.

A little green frog hopped between them, sat looking up at them a moment, and then hopped away.

"All right!" said Saint Peter. "I will!" He turned to the wretched poor man. "Have you always felt this way?"

"Ever since I can remember."

"Try to remember something good. Surely you felt good about something."

The poor man thought about it.

"Well, when I was a boy, there was one summer that I liked. The sun was shining all the time. There was a lot of blue sky and it was warm. I went swimming. That was nice."

He sighed.

"And then?" said Saint Peter.

"Winter came. In more ways than one. I have forgotten now what sunshine is like. I never feel it. I see clouds all day, even if they aren't there. Any river I would swim in would drown me. For me, it is always the middle of winter."

"Thank you," said Saint Peter. He turned to the Lord. "I have it," he said.

"What?" said Jesus.

"The answer to the sufferings of mankind," said Saint Peter. "Eternal summer."

"I don't understand," said Jesus.

A crow sailed through the air above them, with a few flaps of its wings. "Caw," it said, lazily.

"Crimes are caused by poverty. Poverty is caused by want. If you don't want anything, there will be no poverty and no crimes. Understand, Lord?"

"Well," said Jesus.

"You said you'd back me up. I want eternal summer. Now."

Jesus waved his stick.

And the summer came upon them. How wonderful it was. Clouds were few and snow white. The sky was blue and the gentle winds were as sweet and fragrant as your first love. The whole earth seemed to sigh and relax, and turn supple and pliant and delightful to touch.

Saint Peter, Jesus and the wretched poor man turned their faces up to the sun. It beat down upon them with a penetrating, healing warmth. They closed their eyes and let the breeze cool their faces. Their skins turned a soft, leatherish brown. Their bodies stretched.

On the trees and in fields fruit and vegetables began to grow. Within an hour, they were visible everywhere. The wretched poor man cried out and ran to pick some and take to his family.

"This is more like it," said Saint Peter.

There was a lake nearby. With Jesus, Saint Peter strolled down to sit by it, and look at the water. The sunlight and the gentle wind made the tips of the small waves glitter, like a large moving sheet of cloth shot through with diamonds and jewel dust.

Saint Peter and Jesus took off their sandals and walked around the lake. The grass was green everywhere. White and yellow and blue flowers blossomed under their feet. The hot smell of sun-baked pine cones and resin mixed with the cool rippling sounds of a nearby waterfall, to charm them.

Soon Saint Peter was wandering around the lake by himself, gazing. He found himself looking at the world in a way he never had before, as if it, too, was alive and new born, and he—the idea was very strange and astonished him—he was its mother. He shook his head giggling to himself and pictured a mother gazing at her new born child and the child looking up toward her, its face the face of joy.

I am a god in love, thought Saint Peter.

His stomach rumbled. He was hungry, in a sharp, demanding way. It felt delicious.

He asked Jesus to get them something to eat. Jesus waved his stick, and by the lake, on yards of crisp white linen, a picnic appeared spread out over the cool grass. By the glittering lake, in high Hungarian summertime, Jesus and Saint Peter sat down together and dined on delicate fowl, on fresh strawberries, cake and very light wine.

After that, Jesus fell asleep.

Saint Peter sat day dreaming, his stomach full. He dreamed about his wife Perpetua and their lame daughter Petronella, and he hoped they were well and happy in the little house by the sea, where he once lived and fished.

Before he became a god.

The eternal summertime sun beat down on both Jesus and Saint Peter.

Jesus slept. Saint Peter lay staring up into the huge blue sky.

I am in love with the world, he thought.

His knees pulled up. His hands went very loose. His lips had some saliva on them, which turned into drool, and slid down his cheek.

He got up on his hands and knees and crawled down to the lake.

"Fishy?" he said. "Fishy fishy?"

He tried to reach into the water and touch a fish. It swam away. He stayed there, paddling his hands in the water, and smiling blissfully.

His wife Perpetua and his daughter Petronella found him there, by the lake, curled up into a ball, not asleep but watching the grass grow.

"What's happened to him?" said his wife.

"Poppa?" said his daughter.

"Goo, goo," said Saint Peter.

"Stop acting like a baby and get up from there!" said his wife. "We're in danger. Awful things are happening."

"Goo, goo, goo?" said Saint Peter.

"There's a green frog as big as a house," said Petronella. "He's sitting in front of our home, soaking up the lake where you fish. He's getting bigger every day."

"There's a huge tiger," said his wife, "who looks like an oversized cat. He slinks around the side of the house with blood-stained claws."

"A horrible monster the size of a tree trunk is lying over the steps to the house," said Petronella. "It's all greenish-white and grey, like some great caterpillar who has leprosy."

"A huge crow flies over us all day," said Perpetua. "It caws like thunder and tries to pull the roof off the house. It's getting bigger."

In Saint Peter's eternal summer, of course, people shared the earth and its great beauty, with other creatures who ate and grew very quickly: snakes, lizards, scorpions, hippos, pigs, flies, wasps, cockroaches, hornets, hyenas, tapeworms. All mad with joy and growing.

Never mind rabbits.

Or spiders.

"What are we going to do?" said Perpetua. "These things are turning into monsters. They will destroy us."

"Poppa?" said Petronella.

Saint Peter looked up at his wife and daughter.

"Mama?" he said. "Ma-ma?"

"Blockhead!" said Perpetua. "He's turned you into a pudding."

She looked away from the lake and saw Jesus sitting under a tree, watching them. He didn't seem like he wanted to come down and talk to them, but Perpetua called out to him anyway.

"You!" she said. "I want to say something to you!"

Jesus got up and walked away, going around the tree and disappearing behind some more trees.

"No use," said Perpetua. "Look at your father. He's a baby."

And that's what Saint Peter was, too. In Eternal Summer, some grow one way, others grow another. Saint Peter was just a huge bundle of infant love.

He still wanted to touch a fish, and kept trying. A catfish, about twice as big as he ought to have been, slid past and stung him with his gills.

Saint Peter cried. He cried and cried. Like a baby.

Jesus heard him. Everything became what it was again. A chill wind blew. Eternal Summer was no more, and as it went, so Saint Peter came back to himself, uncurled, sat up, stood up, and asked his wife and daughter where Jesus was.

They said they didn't know, and didn't care. Only when they saw a caterpillar on Saint Peter's foot, a little green frog by the lake, a house cat hurrying past them going home, and a plain harmless crow flapping along above them, did they leave.

Saint Peter wasn't quite sure what had happened. He saw Jesus come out of the trees, and when the two met, he asked the Lord what had been happening while he fell asleep by the lake.

"Nothing much," Jesus said.

And never told Saint Peter, who never quite remembered Eternal Summer, either, except now and then when he felt within him a great love for the lazy and beautiful world and something else at the same time that told him, be careful.

And he was.

5

The Good Lord's Curse

My story,
said the Basque Country Frenchman,
is about the Lord, Saint Peter, two drunks, and some Basque
Country farmers.

This was when the Lord and Saint Peter were on a tour of
the world. They came down out of the Spanish mountains
and stood on a ridge not far from here, looking at some farms
in a valley.

What they saw looked good. Crops were growing. The
fields looked dark-loamed and rich. In a settlement they saw
pens, fences, barns, some solid timber-and-plaster homes.
The people looked healthy and hard working. Children ran
about happily.

There was a big sign stuck up on two poles, so it could be
seen from all the fields. It said:

THEY SERVE MOST WHO PROSPER BEST

Saint Peter liked all this very much. He turned to the Lord,
to say, let's visit these good people, but when he did, the Lord
wasn't there.

Jesus had turned right around. He was already moving, climbing a rocky slope just behind them. Saint Peter saw it led up, high up, toward rough mountain country. He sighed, and followed the Lord.

They hadn't climbed more than a mile when clouds gathered. The air got cold and damp. It was going to rain.

"Lord, where are we going?" said Saint Peter. "It looked so nice in that valley."

Jesus pointed to an outcropping of stone, shadowed by the coming dusk.

"What's up there?" said Saint Peter.

"Let's go see," said Jesus.

And off he went. Saint Peter, grumbling, scrambled after him. Halfway to the big rock, night caught them. Gusts of a raw wind swept the slope.

Behind the outcropping, the land leveled out. Through the wind-blown rain, Saint Peter saw a light flickering about a hundred yards inside a stand of scrawny scrub pine. It was in a shack of some kind.

When they reached it, they were wet and their feet were muddy. Their hair was plastered down over their faces. They looked a miserable sight, but so did the shack they saw through the rain.

Its walls were all split and warped and twisted. Its frail timber was chinked together not by plaster or even hard clay, but by dried mud held together by sticks and weeds. It leaned way over on one side, and way in on the other. You couldn't call it a house. There wasn't even a dog around the place to bark at them."

"Knock," said Jesus.

Saint Peter did, gently. He didn't want to knock in the door. In a minute, it creaked open.

Faces. That's all they could see. One on top of the other, filling up the crack in the doorway, like buttons on a coat. Big ones, little ones, all staring out at Jesus and Saint Peter.

They belonged to the skinniest, puniest passle of farm children Saint Peter had ever seen. Big eyes, hollow cheeks, bony scabby arms. Little white pot bellies sticking out of rags, worn, Saint Peter could tell, and slept in until they fell off.

A man holding up a candle appeared behind the children. He had an unkempt beard and feverish eyes. He was dressed in rags, too.

"What do you want?" the man said.

Saint Peter felt so sorry for these people, he didn't know what to say. Jesus nudged him with an elbow.

"I am Saint Peter, and this is the Lord Jesus. May we come in?"

The man stared at them, with his feverish eyes. "Who?" he said.

"We've been traveling all day," said Saint Peter. "We're tired and hungry and rained on. We need some place to spend the night."

A voice called out, from within the shack. It was blurred and indistinct. Saint Peter couldn't tell what it said. The man with unkempt hair turned and called back into the darkness.

"It's two men saying they are Jesus and Saint Peter," he said.

Somebody laughed. "Wait a minute," a voice called out. A woman came to the door.

She moved in lurches, staggering. Under her eyes, as under the eyes of the man and all the children, the skin was dark, and elsewhere sallow. She too was dressed in rags, and now Saint Peter realized that from both the man and the woman came a heavy, fruity odor. It explained the lurching. They were both drunk.

They peered out into the rain.

"Why, sure," said the woman. "You're right. There's Jesus, and there's Saint Peter."

"You think so?" said the man.

"No, but what difference does it make?" said the woman.

"If they want to cut our throats, all they have to do is kick down the door."

Thudding gusts of wind hit the shack. Everything moved. Rain lashed Saint Peter and the Lord.

"We're getting drenched," said Saint Peter.

"Well, come in," said the man.

"Just in time for supper," said the woman, laughing.

Saint Peter said, whew, covered his nose with his hand, and followed Jesus inside.

It was bleak in there. One whole wall of the shack was solid rock, a side of the mountain, wet and cold. In another wall there was a stone fireplace, one window in another, the door in another and that was all. The floor was dirt and clay, littered with corn husks and rushes and connifers to soak up the moisture and cold. A pile of shuck mattresses were stacked in one corner.

A small fire burned meagerly in the stone fireplace, on just a few sticks, each with an inch or so of flame crawling on it. There was an iron pot. One table. Three slat chairs. An old wooden chest. Shelves holding more rags, propped up off the ground by sticks.

This was a hard time family.

"All right, then!" said the woman. "Jesus sits at the head of the table, and Saint Peter I suppose on his right hand, or something like that."

She drank the last of something dark out of a clay mug. She walked unsteadily to the pot that hung over the meager fire. She blinked her eyes and grabbed some wooden bowls from her shelves. She ladled shallow dishes two-thirds up with sour, lukewarm soup. She cut everyone a thumb's width of stiff, stale bread.

There were seven children. They each came by and got the same portion as the grownups. They went to a corner, where they sat in a dark circle. They ate muttering and sometimes snarling, like little animals.

Now and then the woman would yell at them.

It was plain squalid. Saint Peter had a hard time eating. This kind of situation got on his nerves. He liked order, calm at the dinner table, and quiet children.

And the food they were eating was garbage.

Jesus didn't seem to mind. He ate the thin soup as if he enjoyed it, smacking his lips. When he was through, he reached down and picked up a little stick that was lying among the corn husks and rushes.

He waved it, ever so gently. Everybody suddenly felt better. Their stomachs were suddenly nourished by the soup they had eaten.

There was a whooshing sound. The sticks in the stone fireplace blazed.

Jesus stood up.

He looked at the children. They were fighting with each other, saying, shut up, leave that alone, yes, no, give it to me, and so forth.

Jesus sat down in the middle of them, and said, "Now, listen."

They looked at him with suspicion and distrust.

He told them a story about a worried peacock. He told them a story about a fat lion. Then he told them a story about two brothers and two sisters lost in a dark wood, who couldn't find their way home. The children smiled at the first two stories, but not at the third. One by one, they slid over close to Jesus and listened. Jesus finished his story with hair-raising escapes from waterfalls, storms and monsters, but got the brothers and sisters out of the dark forest, home again, and then he fingered that stick, and waved it gently at his side. Seven children fell down on their mattress beds like empty sacks. Jesus spread worn blankets over them, over the flopped out tangle of arms and legs and the sounds of snoring. Then he came back to the table.

"You see?" he said. "This is Saint Peter. I am the Lord Jesus."

The halos lasted only a second. Then they were gone.

The man and woman tried to get down on their hands and knees. But they were drunk and clumsy about it. Jesus said never mind.

It was an embarrassment. Nobody knew what to say.

Saint Peter finally spoke, sternly.

"What are your names?"

"Jacques," said the man.

"Jeannette," said the woman.

"Are you married?"

They hung their heads in shame. They were a sorry sight. Jacques, with his gaunt face, hair and beard all unkempt. Jeannette, bone thin, lines running deep in her face, with a crazy laugh and shrill yell. They went with that shack, all right. And there they stood, before Saint Peter.

"Do you go to church?"

"No," said Jacques.

"No wonder you're in a mess," said Saint Peter.

"It wasn't always this way," said Jacques. "We thought we were like everybody else at first. But we stayed home more and more."

"And drank," said Saint Peter.

"Yes," said Jeannette. "Before we knew it, we were living up here with our children, alone."

"Do you fight?" asked Saint Peter. "Beat each other, and the children?"

"Sometimes," they admitted. They turned to Jesus.

"What happened to us, Lord?" they asked him.

Jesus said he didn't know exactly. Life can be mysterious and sad.

It was another embarrassment. Since Jesus evidently ruled out sermons on the matter, Saint Peter didn't know what to say. Jacques and Jeannette didn't know what to say, either.

The only question left was what tribute this miserable hovel could pay to the Lord and his Apostle who had condescended to visit it. There was an obligation to do something.

So Jacques went to the shelves propped up by sticks. There was a small box there, locked. He opened it and took out a small clay jar. He set it carefully on the table. Jeannette put down four clay cups. Jacques drew a thick cork from the neck of the jar.

He poured half a finger of brandy into each cup, and handed them out.

"We don't mean to insult you," he said. "But this is the best thing we have."

Saint Peter was about to say, put it away, man, that's what's caused your trouble in the first place, when he caught the glance from Jesus.

"It will do," said Jesus. He lifted his cup in a salute.

"To this house," said the Lord.

There was nothing for Saint Peter to do but the same. He took a sip. It was awful. It tasted like sulfur.

But soon Jacques was leaning comfortably against the stone wall, his shame forgotten. Jeannette relaxed, too, and was smiling at Jesus. Saint Peter realized they were all sitting in considerable comfort, hands curled around their cups, watching the fire, which began to warm them.

It was Jesus who started it.

"Know what it means when you stumble over a stone?"

"No, Lord," said Jacques. "What?"

"On that spot a musician lies buried."

Jacques and Jeannette stared at each other. Jacques got a barrel from a corner, and sat next to Jesus.

"Know the cure for leprosy?"

Jesus shook his head.

"You have to wash your skin in the blood of a man whose life you have saved."

Jesus considered that.

So did Saint Peter.

"Where did you hear that?" he said.

"Around," said Jacques. "I know a man who claims you

can teach anything. He says he taught cats to hold candle-sticks."

"He did?" said Jesus. "What for?"

"So he could turn a mouse loose, Lord, and see what happened. He did."

"And?" said Jesus.

"They dropped the candlesticks, and went after the mouse. They learn, his decision was, but they forget."

Saint Peter thought this was the dumbest talk he'd ever heard. He couldn't understand why Jesus had a sparkle in his eyes, or why Jacques and Jeannette did, too.

It was like the three of them were taking a few idle throws before some kind of a ball game.

"A foolish man had two sons," said Jeannette. "One was a thief and tried to steal everything he had. The other was a killer and tried to murder him. What to do? He loved his sons. He sent them to school. One became a lawyer and the other a doctor."

Saint Peter waited for what came next, but nothing did. Jesus sipped his brandy.

"A blind man and a hunchback robbed a merchant," said Jacques. "They sat dividing the spoils. They soon fell out. The blind man said the hunchback was cheating him. The hunchback said the blind man wasn't really blind. The hunchback rubbed dirt in the blind man's eyes. This gave the blind man back his sight. The blind man then beat the hunchback so hard, he broke his hump, and the hunchback stood before the blind man tall and handsome. They both lived happily ever after."

Saint Peter looked out the one window of the shack at the rain coming down. He tried to put the blind man and the hunchback together, but gave up.

Jesus held up his cup. "More brandy?" he said.

"I'm sorry, Lord," said Jacques. "There isn't any."

"Look and see."

Jacques did. The brandy jar was full. He poured Jesus a big

fat dollop. He poured everyone else one, too, and the brandy jar was still full.

It didn't taste like sulfur this time. It was rich and smooth.

Logs grew fresh in the fire, thick ones, sizzling and popping as flames leapt along their backs. Heat flooded the shack. Outside, sheets of rain and gusts of wind passed over the shack without touching it.

Saint Peter yawned. He talked about brandy and rain making him sleepy, and wasn't it about time they all turned in.

"A deaf man," said Jacques, "went to comfort his sick neighbor. He went to the man's bed, and said, 'How are you?' The sick man said, 'Dying.' The deaf man said, 'Thank God for that. Who's your doctor?' The sick man said, 'Doctor Death! Get out!' The deaf man said, 'He's the best! What medicine did he give you?' The sick man said, 'Poison!' The deaf man said, 'Wonderful. I'll see you tomorrow'."

Saint Peter thought Jacques was not in his right mind. But Jesus was smiling.

"There was once a ghost," said Jesus, "doomed to perform amazing tasks every day, and to frighten men."

Saint Peter couldn't believe his ears. The Lord of all creation was telling a silly story about a ghost who had these phantom things to do, and found them tiresome. He wanted the freedom to stay in one place, and not even haunt that, but do ordinary things.

Not only did Jesus tell this pointless story, he gave an imitation of that ghost howling, cupping his hands in front of his mouth and producing a ludicrous noise. When he finished, Jacques and Jeannette not only grinned, they applauded.

Saint Peter knew that no matter how strange the Lord acted, he followed Jesus, and wanted nothing more than to imitate him.

He knew he had to tell a story, too.

"Listen to this," said Saint Peter.

He told a story he remembered from his childhood, How the Mole Got His Tail. But he forgot the part where the mole gives up his eyes for his beautiful tail, didn't understand his own story, had to admit it, and gave up.

Jacques, Jeannette and Jesus were very polite. They said it was very interesting. Then, eyes shining, they plunged into the telling of their own again.

Logs burned. The jar stayed full of brandy. Rain and wind went past the house, leaving it dry. There was more thunder and lightning. It only made them feel safe.

Jacques told, The Moon Frog, The Cornfield Bed, and The Breaking of the Stone of Patience.

Jeannette told, The Water Man, Prince Unexpected, Immortal Bony, and The Ogre Schoolmaster.

Jesus told, The Boy Who Could Not Shudder, Our King In Lethargy, and Phantom Funerals.

Saint Peter knew this had gone far enough. He had to stop it. With something strong. Their own medicine. Something with a punch.

He had it.

"Listen to this," said Saint Peter. "Once upon a time, there was a Sailor and a Parrot."

He didn't see Jesus close his eyes, or Jacques and Jeannette put their hands over their mouths.

"The Sailor sold the Parrot to the Queen. She kept him in her bedroom, in a golden cage. He had everything he wanted. He grew vain and lazy. One day the Queen came naked out of her bath. The Parrot said, 'Whew-o! I see your ass!' The Queen opened the golden cage, pulled the Parrot out by his neck, and throttled him. She gave him to a servant who threw him on the garbage pile outside the Queen's kitchen. He lay there with his neck wrung, but still alive, when a scrawny Chicken came flying out of the kitchen window, plucked bare, neck wrung, and landed on the garbage pile beside the Parrot. The Parrot thought a minute, whistled, and said to the Chicken, 'Whew-o! Whose ass did you see?"

Saint Peter then slapped his knees. He laughed and laughed until his face was red and he choked and gasped.

Jesus, Jeannette and Jacques waited patiently until Saint Peter stopped laughing.

When he did, Jeannette told, The Lady Who Gave Birth To A Rat. Thunder crashed. In the rain outside, winds howled like beasts.

Saint Peter's skin crawled.

Jacques told a tale from the life of the hero, Sir Ever. It was about the death of his son, Sir Now. Sir Now got a maiden named Selma with child. When Selma told Sir Now she was going to have a baby, he laughed at her. Selma's three brothers were listening at the window, and when Sir Now laughed at her, they came in and killed him with sickles. Selma made a chair from his bones, a mattress from his skin, a goblet from his skull, beer from his blood, candles from his fat, wicks from his hair, pies from his flesh, and soup from his fingers. Then she invited his father, Sir Ever, to dinner.

Saint Peter choked, coughed, swallowed, and then had the hiccoughs.

Sir Ever was suspicious. He came to Selma's house, but when she asked him to eat the meal she had prepared for him, he wanted to know who she was. She answered him with a riddle.

Jacques sang the riddle song the betrayed Selma sang Sir Ever. It went like this:

I sit with my love-o,
I drink with my love-o,
I cook with my love-o,
I sleep with my love-o,
My love is my light-o.

I'll give you a pint of wine-o,
When you read my riddle right-o.

Then Jacques told how Sir Ever guessed Selma's riddle, and drew his famous sword. Her brothers rushed in, and he killed them first before he cut off Selma's head.

Then Sir Ever wept bitterly for his evil son, touching the bone chair, lifting the burning candles, and smelling the simmering soup.

This reminded Jesus of Flowering Cholera, and Jeannette of The Catfish God.

They sank into the night, telling wild stories.

Saint Peter sat in his chair wishing he was somewhere else. He gave up trying to stop them.

But it was hard to take. Saint Peter didn't mind a story, even if it was made up. But it ought to have a point to it. It ought to be about life the way life really is. He really did mind tales about people eating other people, and rats born from ladies instead of babies, and impossible heroes who never existed, with names like Sir Ever.

Soon he just wasn't listening to them any more.

That is, until Jeannette said, "Anybody want to hear a Jesus Tale?"

Saint Peter heard that, all right.

"A *what*?" he said.

"Tell one," said Jesus.

"You're sure?" said Jeannette.

"Wait a minute," said Saint Peter.

"Tell it," said Jesus.

So Jeannette told, Saint Peter's Divorce, in which Saint Peter is so miserable at home, he asks Jesus to give him a divorce and Jesus says only if Saint Peter will marry the next woman they meet on the road, and Saint Peter says yes, anything, and of course, the next woman down the road is the ugliest poor creature anybody ever saw. Saint Peter begs off until the next woman down the road, and she is beautiful but mean as the devil, and the next isn't able to talk until Jesus takes a nail from a coffin and sets it against a back tooth and hammers the tooth out, and she talks and talks and can't stop, until Saint Peter begs off her too and goes back to his wife.

This time Saint Peter sat in his chair stiff with resentment. But Jesus was laughing, so what could he do?

Then Jesus told, Jesus, Saint Peter, the Goose and the Bean, and it made Jacques and Jeannette laugh until the tears ran down their cheeks.

And Saint Peter wondered then, a little bitterly, why it was he was always the fool in these matters, no matter how right he actually was. He could see them smiling at him. He felt foolish, as always. He didn't want to make a fuss. But he still did wonder why Jesus provoked him so often, crossed him, got him into positions where he always did the wrong thing, as if he was some sort of big booby on a string Jesus loved to guide and fool.

Why are we sitting up here, in this miserable shack, Saint Peter wondered. Why aren't we down in that valley, with those good healthy farmers?

Jesus filled his cup with brandy.

"Well, one more," said Jesus. "Does anybody know Old Man Joseph the Carpenter?"

Jacques and Jeannette said they both did.

"Tell it," said Jesus.

And so they did, how Joseph the Carpenter was an old man when he met Mary, eighty-nine, in fact, and she only fifteen, who didn't want to marry a young man. How hard he was on her, never believing the wise men and the shepherds and the star were anything but an accident. How furious he got whenever Mary said Jesus was anything special, but how he taught Jesus everything he knew about the world. How because Mary did believe Jesus was something special indeed, Jesus had great troubles as a boy. He wouldn't obey his teachers. He talked back. He looked right through grown-up people. Townsfolk in Nazareth became afraid Jesus had charms and spells and was a Child Terror. Joseph and Jesus had a terrible fight then, and with Mary standing helplessly by, the awful family squalor unfolded itself. Joseph hit Jesus in the face and Jesus hit him back, knocked the old man's crutches out from under him, so that Joseph fell down and didn't know where he was. It was that very night that Joseph died. Outside his house, he saw Azrael, the Angel of Death, with his minions all in black who stood waiting behind him. And finally Joseph became afraid, his great common sense deserted him. He looked at his son, and said he knew the boy was a holy child, and was killing him with his great powers. Then Joseph said he wasn't good enough to be the father of Jesus, that he hoped Jesus would not hate him. He was only the boy's daddy, and a poor foolish one at that. Then Joseph pointed to the wall and told Jesus to look out a window and see what was out there, to tell him the truth, as any good son must, when his father lies dying. Jesus didn't know what to do. He looked out the window, and saw nothing there, but Joseph described Azrael and his minions and how they come for the dead and wanted to know the truth, had they come for Joseph now or not. And Jesus, who was only a boy, was never so frightened in his life, but he saw what he had to do. He stood by Joseph and he said, yes, he saw them all there, Azrael the Angel of Death with his great sword and all the rest of them, and yes, it was true they had come for Joseph, but first they would wait, because he was Jesus the son of Joseph the Carpenter, and so commanded them. They would wait while he paid his father his respect. They would wait while he told him all was well, no fires would burn him, and the seas of demons would be calm. So when Joseph died, in peace, Jesus wept, and kissed the hands that had slapped him.

When the story was told, the fire was going out, and Jesus did not make it burn any longer. The brandy was all gone. The storm outside had passed. The night was quiet and black.

Jesus stared, in silence, at the dying fire.

Saint Peter said, "But none of that happened, did it?"

A few red embers glowed through the ashes. Jesus looked at Saint Peter, sitting in shadow, his big hands crossed on his lap, the country fisherman Jesus loved to fool, who might have been easily taken for a country carpenter instead.

"Of course not," said Jesus, softly.

In the morning, when Jesus and Saint Peter were leaving, Jeannette was in the back yard, washing the family rags in a battered tin tub.

"What this morning you first begin," said Jesus softly, "will not stop until tonight."

They said goodbye, and went off down the road.

Soon Jeannette was calling Jacques, and the children, to come at once. Her hands were tingling and felt wonderful and strong and she couldn't stop washing the clothes that came out of that tub. Work clothes, Sunday clothes, hunting clothes, sleeping clothes, lace handkerchiefs and gaily dyed bandanas, furlined gloves, elegant velvet dresses, heavy winter robes, thick warm socks, everything came soft and sweet smelling and dried at once in a huge growing pile on the ground at her feet.

This lasted all day. Everybody heard about the bottomless tub of clothes, about Jesus and Saint Peter and everybody wondered when they would come again.

They didn't, for five years. And when they did come

again, Saint Peter insisted they spend the night in the valley with the farmers whose sign still proclaimed, THEY SERVE MOST WHO PROSPER BEST.

Dinner on that night was thick bean and bacon soup, meat and fish too, and good red wine, bread like cake with cheese and strawberries and plenty of fresh milk. Then pie.

The farmers' children gave a pageant about Jesus riding into Jerusalem. A boy, playing Jesus, came in on the backs of two other boys playing the mule. The children clapped their hands and sang a song. The farmers' wives gave the boy playing Jesus fresh flowers, and he gave them to Jesus and Saint Peter.

There was a dance for the Lord.

Jesus changed his flowers into beer, and sat sipping it, saying not a word.

The next morning, when they were ready to go, Saint Peter said to Jesus, "You must do it for them, too."

"The clothes?"

"They know about it. You have to."

"I won't."

They had an argument.

"Now, listen," said Saint Peter, finally. "I stayed up half that night, listening to those crazy wild stories. I was nice to your kind of people. You be nice to mine."

What could Jesus say after that? When the farmers gathered around to wish them goodbye, and it was obvious they expected something, Jesus said, "What this morning you first begin, will not stop until tonight."

They hardly waited until Jesus and Saint Peter were off down the road before they all gathered around the richest farmer.

"You all know what to do," he said. "Everybody has his purse. You start right now, counting money out of your purses. The money, like those clothes, will keep coming out, all day long. Everybody ready?"

They all were. But the farmer stopped a minute, and thought.

"Wait," he said. "We should all go into the woods and relieve ourselves first. That way we won't have to stop later, or waste any time counting money."

All the farmers agreed. They ran into the woods.

On the road, not far away from the valley, Jesus and Saint Peter looked up and saw the high ridge they'd climbed five years before.

An old woman in a floppy hat was leading her cow past them on the road. Saint Peter stopped her.

"There is a man and a woman who live up there," he said, pointing. "With many children. Do you know who I mean?"

"Yes, Saint Peter," said the old woman. "They died."

"Both?"

"Yes. They were troubled. They drank. The mother caught pneumonia. The father threw himself off a cliff. The children were given out to strangers."

When the old woman was gone, he turned to Jesus. "You see?" he said.

Then Jesus stared angrily at him, and pointed back down the road, toward the valley. Dark swirling storm clouds swept over it, and as the Lord pointed, rain poured out of them, lightning flashed, the most ominous of thunders rolled. Cries and moans and furious shouts of many farmers rose and fell against the wind. They were all still in the woods, fighting their bodies, their bowels giving and giving, and wouldn't stop. They remembered then that what they first began would go on all day, and in a tangle of fury they were amazed at their own stupidity.

Jesus then pointed to that high slope above the ridge, where of a flimsy shack of drunkards who told stories against the night, only the broken stones of a fireplace and the mouldering walls of a home remained. There the sun was shining brightly.

When Saint Peter looked again at Jesus, around the head of the Lord, his halo was blazing.

Then Jesus stomped down the road, with Saint Peter following, but very carefully, knowing that the passions of God are deep and unfathomable, and even if he, Saint Peter himself, demanded the truth, he wouldn't get it.

And that, brave friends, is the legend of the Good Lord's Curse.

6

Happy Jeanne, Good Natured Billy, Nasty Johnny, and Deadly Marie

When Jesus was on earth,
said the Irishman,
he and Saint Peter got along most of the time, but not always.

One fight they had was over a girl. Two girls. Let me tell you about it.

They kept passing through a certain town with a fine, deep well. The first time through, a young girl was at the well, drawing water. She saw Jesus coming, and she offered the Lord a drink of water from her dipper. Jesus took it and thanked her. She gave Saint Peter one, too. The three of them had a nice talk.

This girl was a pleasant, open sort of person, frank and merry. She had a strapping young sweetheart she was going to marry. He was her strong, good-natured Billy. They met him, too.

The next time through this town, there was a different girl at the well. She was sullen and hard-faced. Her eyes were full of suspicion all the time. Her mouth twisted in an ugly way whenever she said anything. It seemed a shadow was always over her face, even in broad daylight.

This girl saw Jesus coming, too. She offered him and Saint Peter nothing at all. In fact, she made them both wait while she drew her own water.

Deadly Marie, she was called. A lanky, pasty-faced boy with a scar down one cheek hung around her. He was her nasty Johnny.

Saint Peter disliked Deadly Marie and her nasty Johnny on sight, but Happy Jeanne and her good natured Billy delighted him. He had a shrewd country eye for a handsome young couple and the good life that could lie ahead of them.

"Look at them, Lord," he said. "Young, in love. Can't keep their hands off each other, and wanting to get married. What babies they'll have!"

Then he looked across the well at deadly Marie and scar-faced Johnny.

"Those two. What trouble they'll have. Sad. But that, too, is God's will. All is well."

And he lectured Jesus and the good people standing around the well on the importance of a good healthy family life.

Jesus didn't interrupt him. He stood listening, scratching his ear with one hand, in a peculiar way.

Saint Peter noticed it.

The next time through the town, they saw that two weddings were taking place. At the same time.

Good-natured Billy was marrying deadly Marie. Scar-faced Johnny was marrying merry Jeanne.

"What happened?" said Saint Peter, flabbergasted.

People in town said it came about very suddenly, right there at the well. Billy and Jeanne began looking away from each other, as if idly curious about nothing much, and so did Marie and Johnny. Billy began edging over to Marie. When she teased and mocked him, in her sharp way, he snorted with pleasure. Johnny slid around to talk with Jeanne. He told her a lot of lies. She told him she admired a man who did what he pleased without asking women if he could or not, and his scar turned pink. So it wasn't long before that sweet girl and that nasty boy, they were crazy about each other. That fine lad and that shrew couldn't take their eyes off each other, either.

"It's going to be a mess," said Saint Peter.

He was right. It was.

Passing through the town that next year or two, Jesus and Saint Peter heard the sad stories. Screaming fights, slovenly drinking, all the awful squalid familiar scenes.

Scar-faced Johnny hit his merry Jeanne once too often, and merry Jeanne put out one of his eyes with a knitting needle. When good-natured Billy stayed out all night drinking, deadly Marie stayed home hating the baby they had right away. When he came home drunk, she scalded him with bitterness.

They came to grief. All were to blame. There was adultery, fury, hysteria, melancholy. They were driven by anger and bewilderment from one day to the next.

One day, when Jesus and Saint Peter were traveling through the town, they met good-natured Billy. It wasn't noon yet, but he was blind drunk.

When he saw Saint Peter, he staggered up to him.

"What happened to us?" he said. "We were going to be so happy."

Saint Peter couldn't answer him.

On the night of his second child's birth, good-natured Billy was knifed in a tavern brawl, and died.

Jesus and Saint Peter went to his funeral. Merry Jeanne was there, weeping. Deadly Marie was there, smiling scornfully at everyone. Scar-faced Johnny, now One-Eyed Johnny, drank from a bottle he hid under his coat, couldn't always see where he was walking, tripped, and fell down twice.

"It seemed so right the other way," said Saint Peter.

Jesus agreed, but without concern.

Saint Peter felt peculiar.

He didn't say anything then. Or when the three lovers left the funeral, and he could see when they walked past, how much they hated each other, themselves, and what had become of them.

He didn't even say anything when he learned that One-Eyed Johnny ran away and left merry Jeanne pregnant. Or when he heard that deadly Marie gave her children away to some farmers, and went to live with a rich old man, as a suspicious sort of nurse, and inherited all his money when he died very quickly.

But when Saint Peter heard that the beautiful merry Jeanne was caught by townsfolk beating and cursing her infant son, that's when he said plenty, and Saint Peter and Jesus had their fight.

It was right out in the middle of that town, where everybody could hear them.

"You did it!" yelled Saint Peter.

"Did what?" yelled Jesus.

They were both flying off the handle.

"How could you be so cruel!" said Saint Peter.

"I don't know what you're talking about!" said Jesus.

"It was all right until you butted in!" said Saint Peter. "And scratched your ear!"

"Scratched my ear?" said Jesus.

"Don't pretend with me!" said Saint Peter. "You know what you did!"

"No, I don't!" said Jesus.

"You made those lovers marry the wrong people!" said Saint Peter.

"Why would I do that?"

"You hate families! You hate people in love with anyone but you!"

"So I scratched my ear and—"

"That's right!"

Jesus was exasperated.

"Life is life!" said Jesus. "What do you want me to do about it? Do you think I'm to blame for everything?"

Saint Peter was furious.

"You've tricked me for the last time! I can't stand your carelessness and your cruelty any longer!"

"Baby!" said Jesus.

"Liar!" said Saint Peter.

That tore it. The Lord and Saint Peter both went too far. They lost all patience with each other. They stood there in the middle of that town glaring at each other. There was nothing to be done.

They turned away, each from the other, in disgust. They walked off a different way. People shook their heads.

Saint Peter went back to his wife, Perpetua, who was wise enough not to say I told you so, and to his lame daughter, Petronella. He lived again in his house by the sea of Galilee, and took up his old profession, fishing. He wouldn't talk about Jesus to any one.

Jesus wandered around preaching, curing the sick, performing miracles now and then, but not often. He wouldn't talk about Saint Peter. He wouldn't let anybody else talk about him. At first it seemed that Jesus wasn't bothered by the quarrel they'd had, but there was something missing. I mean, his preaching was just as good, people were still astonished by him, but there was something light-hearted and happy gone out of it. Not many noticed, but a few did.

Months went by. It was taken for granted that they were finished with each other. Saint Peter was really too much of a family man for Jesus, people said. And the Lord was simply too unpredictable for Saint Peter.

Both seemed content without the other. Men, even if one of them is Jesus Christ, can't get along with each other all the time.

But early one morning, before dawn, when Saint Peter came out of his house with his nets over his shoulder to go fishing, he saw a familiar figure sitting on his upturned fishing boat, back toward him. Saint Peter's blood jumped. It was the Lord.

Jesus was sad. He was sitting on Saint Peter's boat with his shoulders drooping. He was staring idly at the ground, where, with a long stick, he was tracing the outlines of a fish in the sand.

And Saint Peter remembered that was the way Jesus had been when he'd first met him years before, alone, in a desert, and sad like that.

Saint Peter came down from his house to the boat. He slung his nets over the upturned prow. Then, without saying a word, he just sat next to Jesus, and the two of them looked at the lake for awhile.

They watched the great day that dawned above them, and the light as it spread out over the Sea of Galilee.

"I've been thinking," said Saint Peter, deciding that after all, Jesus was the Lord, and could hardly speak first. "I shouldn't get so excited."

"Me, either," said Jesus, quickly.

They made it up. Saint Peter allowed of course he couldn't really blame Jesus for all the messes callow youth and hot blood made of life. Jesus allowed that was true, but on the other hand, he needed men who would stand up to him and let him know what he thought, even when the Lord might not like it, and he hoped Saint Peter would always do that.

They talked the morning by. Saint Peter never did go fishing.

He invited Jesus to lunch. Perpetua, his wife, and Petronella, his lame daughter, both groaned when they saw him coming up the path to the house with Jesus. They knew what it meant. But they saw Saint Peter was smiling, and his lined face had relaxed. He'd been so gloomy, just going fishing with nothing to say at night. There he was, smiling and talking happily with the Lord. So mother and daughter looked at each other and nodded.

They said nothing but welcome, Lord.

For his part, Jesus was very polite to Saint Peter's wife and daughter. He made it a point to praise their solid family life, and lasting love for each other, which not even the great adventures and sacrifices of the Lord's travels could alter. He was very kind to Petronella, and made her laugh and feel gay, and he never looked at her legs or mentioned the affliction that her father could not cure.

They gave him their spare bed, and the next morning early, Jesus and Saint Peter set off traveling again, just the two of them for awhile now, to get to know each other again, preaching, baptizing babies, founding churches and doing good all over their own countryside and in far-off foreign lands.

They just avoided that place with the well.

Not that they didn't have other fights later. Like when Jesus, if they made him mad enough, turned whole towns into lakes.

But that's another story.

7
Saint Peter's Claim

Jesus and Saint Peter,
said the Texan,
appeared one day in front of a chapel down here in south
Texas. It was high noon and hot and nobody was around.
The Chapel looked neglected. Doors hung off hinges.
Chickens walked in and out. Goats peed on the walls. Inside,
it was filthy dirty.

The Padre was lying in a pew, dead drunk.

Saint Peter got mad.

"Gutbucket!" he said. "Souse! What do you mean, lying
here drunk, with the Lord's Chapel a filthy mess!"

He got that Padre up in a hurry.

He fell on his knees before Saint Peter and the Lord. He
begged them to forgive him.

He was very young. This was his first mission, and in a
foreign country. He was not only drunk, but truly miserable,
and ashamed.

"Padre," said Saint Peter. "You're forgiven. Just tell us
how things got so bad."

"This is Texas," said the Padre.

"So?" said Saint Peter.

"I come from the old country, like you and the Lord. People here just aren't like that. You can't make them do anything they don't want to do, and you can't stop them from doing what they want to do."

"You can't, eh?" said Saint Peter.

"They have nothing against religion," said the Padre. "They just don't have time for it. They're too busy."

Saint Peter glared at him. "Doing what?" he said.

The Padre kept blushing. Not only was he young, he was shy.

"Fornicating," he said, in a whisper.

"My goodness, Padre," said Saint Peter. "Don't you read your Bible? People are human, in Texas like everywhere else. Of course they fornicate. So?"

"You don't understand," said the Padre.

He told Saint Peter and the Lord the history of Texas fornication. How in the old days, there were just a lot of men camping out and working hard and drinking hard. They ran over each other with horses and shot each other with pistols to keep from thinking about it too much. Then a Chapel was built, and a Padre put in it. Women came from big cities, and went to Chapel. The whores went to Chapel too, and reformed, some of them. When people married, they did that in Chapel, and when they had babies, they brought them to Chapel to be baptized. All things prospered. Herds, farms, stores, families, and the Chapel. The old Padre died, and a new one was sent for.

When he arrived, he saw all around him lusty men, and sultry women. They all had hot Texas blood. They had worked hard for a long time, and now they meant to enjoy themselves.

So when they saw the new Padre, they laughed at him, and did what they pleased.

"Go look at the way they strut around town, ogling each other. It's awful! And the things they say!"

A more miserable Padre Saint Peter never saw.

"So I drink!" the young Padre said.

His lips trembled. His hands shook. His eyes got a funny light in them.

"Husbands won't touch their married wives! Wives won't touch their married husbands! Little children play house in the barns. For hours!"

"He's a wreck," said Saint Peter.

"Padre," said Jesus. "Do you have bad dreams sometimes, about wives and husbands and what they do to each other and the little children playing in the barn, and so on?"

The Padre was hurt.

"You think I'm imagining everything," he said. "Well, I'm not. It's all true. And so is what the husbands do to the husbands and the wives to the wives."

Saint Peter looked serious then. He gazed down the street of the Texas town, and shook his head.

"It may be," he said.

"What may be?" said Jesus.

"The Padre's right," said Saint Peter. "In spite of his youth. I've seen it before. Chapels abandoned. Priests drinking."

"You think so?" said Jesus.

"Carnal confusion," said Saint Peter. "Not all that serious."

"You're sure he isn't just baked out by the heat?" said Jesus. "He's a very young man."

"You're a young man, too, Lord," said Saint Peter. "Don't forget that."

"True," Jesus admitted.

"You weren't even married," said Saint Peter. "Let me handle this."

"You?" said Jesus.

"Give me a week and I'll clean the town up."

"A week?"

"One week, with thunder and lightning."

"Why thunder and lightning?"

"When they lie to me. And the Chapel gets named after me."

"All right," said Jesus. "One week."

And the Lord walked out of town.

Saint Peter and the Padre went to work right away, with hammers, nails, paint, brushes, paper, cardboard, plaster and wood. There was a lot of banging and sawing going on inside the Chapel. Texans, passing by, wondered about it, briefly.

The next day at noon the old Chapel bell clanged and banged.

At once Jesus appeared on the Chapel roof, ducking down, so no one would see him.

The whole town turned out, over a hundred Texans, wanting to know what was the matter.

The Padre came out of the Chapel. He was carrying a wooden pedestal. He set the pedestal down in front of the Chapel, turned around and went back in.

"Now, what the hell?" said the Mayor. He was a swarthy, pot-bellied little man, in a cutaway coat and a shiny stovepipe hat he wore all the time. He had a big, sleek handlebar moustache, too.

"Damned if I know," said the Sheriff. He was a tall, lanky, leather-brown mean-looking fellow, with dangerous eyes.

"What's the Padre up to now?" said the Blacksmith. He was the biggest man in town, with a huge belly and great fat arms that were enormous from handling his hammer and tongs, and he smelled like horses and fire.

"That poor little Padre," said the Mayor's wife. She was a whore who reformed when she married the Mayor. She had on a very tight dress, and wore a hat with red turkey feathers in it. "What does he think he's doing?"

The Padre came out of the Chapel again, this time carrying a large box marked ALMS. He set that down next to the pedestal.

"Padre, what's going on?" said the Mayor.

"You'll see," said the Padre.

Saint Peter came out of the Chapel. He was pushing a wheel-barrow, in it a large sign, with something painted on it, and a large black book.

The Padre took the book out of the wheel-barrow and set it on the pedestal.

Saint Peter put the wheel-barrow beside the pedestal, and left it there, with the sign still in it, face down.

The Padre faced the Texans.

"Friends and neighbors," he said, using the right words but stiffly, you know, like a man not sure of his sale, and whether it's going through or not. "We've had a falling out here in Texas, and I'm sorry about it. It is too bad. Chapel is important. Religion is important. Immortal souls are important, too. Something has to be done."

A remark was made then about the Padre sobering up enough to say a prayer, but that was hushed.

"The Lord in heaven knows our troubles," said the Padre. "He has sent Saint Peter himself to Texas to straighten us out."

"Straighten *us* out?" somebody said, but that was hushed, too. The Texans all stared at Saint Peter. He was something to see.

Saint Peter stepped forward.

A little ceremony did seem in order. So the Mayor pushed his wife forward. She took a desert rose out of her hair and gave it to Saint Peter. He thanked her with a frosty smile.

The Blacksmith, always on the look-out for customers,

didn't know whether Saint Peter used a horse or not, but taking no chances, gave him a plug of tobacco, and Saint Peter gave him a frosty smile, too.

The Mayor thought that was enough. "Well, stranger," he said.

"Saint Peter!" said the Padre.

"Well, stranger," said the Mayor again, "Welcome to Texas. We have a lot of old sayings around here we dearly love. They cover a lot of ground."

The Texans nodded, smiling.

"Like this one," said the Mayor. "I'm always glad to see a stranger, so long as he don't tell me how many teeth I got in my mouth."

Then he shook hands with Saint Peter.

"Welcome to Texas," said the Mayor's wife. "If you make your bed right, you can turn over in it more."

She shook hands with him, too, and winked at him.

"Welcome to Texas!" said the Blacksmith. "Don't run all your possums up one little tree!"

"Welcome to Texas," said the Sheriff. "Stranger, I keep the peace here. You make trouble, and you'll wish you were home under Momma's bed, playing with the cat."

The Sheriff didn't shake Saint Peter's hand at all. He was the Law. He wasn't shaking hands with rivals.

Saint Peter gazed thoughtfully at the people of Texas.

On the roof, hand over his mouth, Jesus was laughing.

Saint Peter pointed to the sign in the wheel-barrow. The Padre took it out and hung it by a chain on the Chapel wall, just over the pedestal, the black book and the ALMS box.

The sign read:

SAINT PETER'S TEXAS CHAPEL
SAINT PETER'S TEXAS CLAIM
SAINT PETER'S RIGHTS IN TEXAS
GLORY TO GOD IN TEXAS
SIGN HERE

"What's that?" said the Sheriff.

"Explain it," said Saint Peter.

"Well," said the Padre. He was blushing again.

"Out with it!" said the Mayor.

On the roof, the Lord Jesus had both hands on his mouth to stop himself from laughing.

"Every time—you—I mean—a man and a woman—or anybody—every time—or even by themselves—every time—when they—when they—"

"Fuck, Padre?" said the Sheriff. "That what you're trying to say? Fuck?"

"You pay Saint Peter a dollar. That's it."

On the roof, Jesus was pinching himself.

"What did he say?" said the Mayor.

"Saint Peter," said the Padre. "You pay Saint Peter."

"No," said the Mayor. "The other part."

"It costs a dollar?" said the Blacksmith.

"That's right."

"Even with me?" said the Mayor's wife.

"That's right," said the Padre.

The Texans laughed at that. It was silly. The Blacksmith laughed the loudest. He liked to brag about how many times he did it in one day, and with how many women.

"Your dollar goes in there," said the Padre, pointing to the ALMS box. "Then you write about it in here." He opened the pages of the big black book. They were all blank. He showed them a receptacle next to it holding a bottle of ink and goose-quill pens.

"Write what in your god damned book?" said the Sheriff.

"Well, the names of the participants, the time and place of the event," said the Padre. "Plus a brief but accurate description of what happened."

The Texans grinned and winked at each other. This was just a hoot, that's all.

"Mr. Mayor," said the Sheriff, shaking his head with

amusement. "Do you want to take action, or shall I?"

"I'm leaving it to you, Sheriff," said the Mayor, putting his arm around his wife's pretty shoulders. "Show Saint Peter what's none of his business."

The Sheriff drew his six-shooter.

"Saint Peter, you have come into our town with the nerve to tell us we pay you a dollar every time we have bodily pleasure any way at all. Is that right?"

"That's right," said Saint Peter.

"Then I am telling you, get out of our town pronto," said the Sheriff.

And he fired his six-shooter into the air.

Saint Peter looked up at the sky.

A crash of thunder came upon them. A bolt of chain lightning ripped the ground at the Sheriff's feet, making a smoking hole six feet deep.

"Drop those guns," said Saint Peter.

"I told you he was Saint Peter," said the Padre.

"Take your pleasure," said Saint Peter. "But pay for it. If you lie to me, you know what will happen."

There was a rumble of thunder in the sky.

The Texans knew this shoot-out was over. They dropped their guns into the wheel-barrow.

The Mayor and the Sheriff asked Saint Peter respectfully if they might have a conference.

Saint Peter agreed.

A young Mexican woman approached Saint Peter timidly. She fell on her knees at his feet.

"San Pedro!" she said.

"Yes, my child?" said Saint Peter.

"My name is Carolita."

A man knelt beside her.

"My name is Manuel," he said. "I am her faithful husband."

"I am glad to hear it," said Saint Peter. "You don't run around fornicating."

"Oh, no, San Pedro," said Manuel.

"We have been married for five happy years, San Pedro," said Carolita. "But no children."

"She is barren, San Pedro," said Manuel.

"Or he is, San Pedro," said Carolita.

"She is," said Manuel.

"What can we do, San Pedro?" said Carolita.

"Fertility," said Saint Peter, "is a gift of God. Manuel, send your wife to the Chapel every day, at noon exactly, to pray for her baby, in the name of Saint Peter. Will you do that?"

"Yes, San Pedro," said Manuel.

"Thank you, San Pedro," said Carolita.

"God bless you both," said Saint Peter.

The Mayor and the Sheriff came forward.

"Saint Peter," said the Mayor.

"We have a proposition to put to you," said the Sheriff.

"All right," said Saint Peter. "But everybody else go in the Chapel with the Padre, to clean it up. I want things nice in there, where I will see you all, Sunday morning."

There was a slight rumble of thunder and a quick flash of lightning.

The Texans went into the Chapel. The Mayor and the Sheriff stayed outside with Saint Peter.

"We'll support your proposition, if you'll support ours," said the Mayor.

"But we are elected officials," said the Sheriff.

"We don't have thunder and lightning like you do," said the Mayor.

"We have to get elected again this year," said the Sheriff.

"We want to support you, Saint Peter," said the Mayor. "But suppose somebody got elected in our place?"

"Let us put it to you straight," said the Sheriff. "You have access to the Lord. And the Lord knows everything."

"What's in the future," said the Mayor.

"To make us look good," said the Sheriff.

"You back us and we back you," said the Mayor. "See?"

They waited while Saint Peter made up his mind.

"Have you fellows noticed," Saint Peter said finally, "how men are made up of twos of everything?"

The Mayor and the Sheriff thought that over.

"Twos?" they said.

"Two eyes, two ears, two hands, two feet and so on," said Saint Peter.

"Well, yes," said the Mayor.

"So?" said the Sheriff.

"So why shouldn't men have two stomachs?" said Saint Peter. "And two dongs?"

The Mayor and the Sheriff stared bug-eyed at Saint Peter. Their jaws dropped open.

"Two stomachs?" said the Mayor.

"Two dongs?" said the Sheriff.

"You mean we could promise them that?" said the Mayor.

Saint Peter winked at them. They grabbed his hand, and shook it hard.

"Thank you, Saint Peter!" said the Sheriff.

"Praise the Lord!" said the Mayor.

They went into the Chapel to make sure everybody was working hard, and there'd be no mistake about following Saint Peter's new legislation to the letter.

Saint Peter watched them go.

"They were strangers," he said to himself, smiling. "So I took them in."

And he had a pleasant walk, to see the rest of the town.

On the Chapel roof, the Lord was on his back, laughing.

In a week, that Chapel was whitewashed, had new windows, and flower beds outside the door. Sunlight glinted off the bell in the tower, which was polished bright and shining.

Work still went on inside the Chapel but outside it looked wonderful.

Saint Peter stood outside the Chapel, congratulating the Padre. The week was over. The candles were burning softly in the Chapel now, and everybody came once a day to do something helpful.

"How's the plastering and painting inside?"

"Almost done."

"Good. What are you so nervous about?"

"Oh, nothing," said the Padre.

It hadn't been easy. A lot of strong-willed Texans had to make considerable sacrifices. On the other hand, that book became interesting reading. People learned how much the Blacksmith's reputation meant, since he had to pay more dollars than anyone, just to keep it up. How the old folks couldn't always be sure when they qualified and when they didn't, and how the young people, getting as much as they could for their dollar, wore themselves out. They were fascinated to find out that the Mayor's dignified father liked geese. That the Sheriff's deputy used melons in some strange way, while his wife hit him with a bull whip. That the Mayor's wife went off once a week to visit her Uncle Mary and Aunt Joe.

These combinations made spicy reading, but in general it was pretty much what you'd think, and people laughed about it a lot more than they condemned it. It was hard to get really wrathful over the things they read in that book.

And we don't need to count every tooth in the head here.

People had what they needed. Carnality was kept in bounds, and there were plenty of dollars to fix up that Chapel.

Saint Peter had tamed that Texas town.

But that doesn't explain why the Padre was so nervous and

upset when they stood together outside the Chapel at the end of the week.

Saint Peter picked up the ALMS box. It was full of silver dollars. He picked up the black book.

It was full of writing.

When he saw Saint Peter open the book the Padre said, "For shame, Saint Peter!"

"Hush, man. We deserve a little innocent fun. What happened today?"

He handed the book to the Padre.

"Today?" said the Padre, turning pale.

"Read me one or two."

"I can't!"

The Padre gave the book back to Saint Peter and ran into the Chapel.

"What's the matter with him?" wondered Saint Peter. He started reading. He chuckled. Then he came to the last entry made that day. This is what it said:

> TODAY I HAD MANUEL'S WIFE CAROLITA
> BEHIND THE HIGH ALTAR AND PAID
> MYSELF A SILVER DOLLAR SIGNED SAINT PETER

Saint Peter blinked. He read it twice.

He was livid. He dashed into the Chapel, climbed to the tower, and rang that bell as it had never been rung before.

The Texans dropped what they were doing, and got to the Chapel fast.

Where Saint Peter was waiting for them.

"All right!" said Saint Peter. "Who wrote this?"

He read them the blasphemous entry from the book.

"Ohhhh!" said the Texans. They were shocked.

But nobody admitted doing it.

"Manuel!" said Saint Peter. "Carolita!"

"Si, San Pedro?" said Manuel.

"Si, San Pedro?" said Carolita.

"Who wrote this in my book?"

"Why, San Pedro," said Manuel. "We thought you did."

"Me?" said Saint Peter. "Why should I write such a thing in my own book?"

"Because is true," said Manuel.

"What's true?"

"You had my wife at noon, behind the High Altar."

"I *what*?"

"So my wife says, San Pedro."

"Carolita!" said Saint Peter.

"You did. Don't you remember?"

Saint Peter was flabbergasted.

"Be careful! You saw the thunder, the lightning. Tell the truth!"

"I *am* telling the truth!" insisted Carolita. "You had me in the Chapel, behind the—"

Saint Peter threw both hands up into the air.

"Thunder!" he said. "Lightning!"

The sun was shining. Birds were singing.

"I don't see one cloud in the whole blue sky," said the Sheriff.

"San Pedro," said Manuel. "You told my wife to come at noon to pray for baby."

"That's right," said Saint Peter. "I did. So?"

"So," said Carolita, "I did every day, and today you had me and I'm pregnant. Not that I mind. I'm happy, San Pedro. Of course, my husband—"

"I am not so happy, San Pedro."

Saint Peter couldn't believe his ears.

"Liars!" he said.

"Then where's the thunder and lightning?" said the Mayor.

"I don't know," said Saint Peter.

The Mayor's wife stepped forward. "I do!" she said.

The Padre tried to stop her. "No!" he said.

But she brushed by him. "I mean to speak up!" she said, firmly. "I mean to tell everybody what I saw in that Chapel!"

"For God's sake," said the Padre.

"Today at noon," said the Mayor's wife, "I was taking lilacs into the Sanctuary. I heard moans and cries of pleasure. They came from behind the High Altar."

"Villains!" said Saint Peter. "Did you recognize the voices?"

"Please," said the Padre.

"I couldn't see them," said the Mayor's wife. "But the man was saying, *Oh Carolita! Oh yes, Carolita!*"

"That's right," said Carolita, smiling. "He was."

"The wretches!" said Saint Peter.

"The woman was saying, over and over, *O Saint Peter! O Saint Peter!*"

"That's right," said Carolita.

The Texans shook their heads.

"It wasn't me!" said Saint Peter. He pointed to the Mayor's wife. "She's lying, too!"

"No, she isn't," said the Padre. He took a deep breath, and confronted Saint Peter. "I was right behind her. I heard it, too."

Saint Peter was aghast. "Padre," he said. "Think about your immortal soul."

"I have," said the Padre, bitterly. "All day. And how when you first came here, you kicked me around, and all I'd done was drink a bottle of wine. Now I'm standing up to you! I'm telling the truth! And so are they!"

And he pointed to Manuel, Carolita and the Mayor's wife.

Things didn't look good for Saint Peter.

"San Pedro!" demanded Manuel. "What have you done to my wife?"

"I told her to come to Chapel and maybe she'd get pregnant!"

"She did!" said Manuel. "By you!"

"No, she didn't!" said Saint Peter.

"Yes, I did!" said Carolita.

The Texans began to boo and hiss Saint Peter.

"Stop it!" said Saint Peter. "This is ridiculous. If it happened today at noon how can she know she's pregnant?"

"I know the signs!" said Carolita. "Wax won't stick to my fingers. That's one. When I tie a knot in a string, it comes undone. That's two. I can't move my bowels. That's three. I'm pregnant."

That Texas crowd wondered about the week just past. Those dollars. They burned up, thinking about Saint Peter and Carolita behind the High Altar and how there wasn't any thunder and lightning.

"String him up!" somebody shouted.

There was a roar of approval.

"By his dong!" shouted the Sheriff.

"By his dong?" said the Mayor.

"Two stomachs and two dongs?" said the Sheriff.

"By his dong!" shouted the Mayor. "Damn right!"

"Now, wait," said the Padre. "He is Saint Peter."

"Hush up, Padre," said the Sheriff. "Or we'll string you up by yours. Somebody get a rope!"

"Grab him!" yelled the crowd.

Saint Peter felt a lot of rough Texas hands on him.

This was no joke.

"Lord!" said Saint Peter. "Where are you?"

So finally it wasn't thunder or lightning that stopped the Texans. It was what you see when you look at the sun too long.

When it went away, Jesus stood in the middle of the street. With him stood two angels. They were both dressed in white. One of them was a middle-aged woman, and the other a girl, leaning on ivory crutches.

"Who's this?" said the Mayor.

"The Lord Jesus," said the Padre.

"My wife," said Saint Peter. "My daughter."

By this time the Mayor was ready for anything.

"Look here," he said. "Everybody loves the Lord. And Saint Peter's family we got no quarrel with. But this is a hanging."

"Best stay out of it, Lord," said the Sheriff.

"What did he do?" said Jesus.

"He had carnal relations in the Chapel," said the Mayor.

"With my wife!" said Manuel.

"Now I'm pregnant," said Carolita.

"It's not true!" said Saint Peter. "I didn't do it!"

Jesus turned to Carolita.

"Carolita?" said the Lord.

Carolita knelt before Jesus.

"Nuestro Señor. As I hope for heaven, it is the truth."

"But it's not!" said Saint Peter.

"String him up!" said the Texans.

Somebody threw the Sheriff a rope, with a mean little hangman's noose tied at one end.

"Just a minute," said the Lord. "Everybody should get what they deserve, including Saint Peter. But if this deed was done in the Chapel, I want to see where. Then do as you wish."

"He *is* the Lord," said the Padre.

"Well," said the Mayor.

"But only for a minute," said the Sheriff, slinging the rope over his back.

Grumbling, the Texans went into the Chapel with Jesus. Behind them, swinging herself forward on her ivory crutches, came the angel Petronella, with her angel mother Perpetua.

They all went inside the Chapel.

Carolita went behind the High Altar and brought out a large piece of paint-spattered canvas. She spread it out and dropped it on the floor, before everyone.

"On that," she said.

Everybody shook their heads.

"What do you have to say for yourself?" Jesus said to Saint Peter.

"It never happened," said Saint Peter.

"Yes, it did," said Carolita.

"String him up!" said the Sheriff.

"Why was the cloth there?" said Jesus.

"It's a painter's cloth," said the Padre. "He covers things here while he paints the ceiling."

"Painter?" said Jesus.

"Yes, Lord," said the Padre. "Working on the Chapel."

"I got him the job," said the Mayor. "He's an orphan boy who does odd jobs. His name is Little Buddy."

"Where is Little Buddy now?" said Jesus.

"He may be up there," said the Padre.

Above them, close to the ceiling, hung a scaffold.

"Little Buddy!" said the Padre.

The scaffold moved. Little Buddy stared down at them. He was covered with plaster dust and flecks of white paint.

"What are you doing up there?" said Jesus.

"Painting and plastering, Lord," said Little Buddy.

"Those arms," said Carolita.

"Were you up there today at noon?" said Jesus.

"Yes, Lord."

"Did you see anything?"

"No, Lord," said Little Buddy.

"Little Buddy," said the Mayor.

"That's the Lord talking to you," said the Sheriff.

"You'll hang me," said Little Buddy.

"No, we won't," said the Mayor. "I swear by the Lord Jesus, nobody will hang you. All right, Lord?"

Jesus said that was all right.

"Well," said Little Buddy. "Every day here for a week, a good looking woman comes into the Chapel at noon."

"His chin," said Carolita. "Those hands."

"Praying, *Help me, Saint Peter. My husband is an idiot.*"

"What's that?" said Manuel.

"*He can't make a baby, Saint Peter and I want a baby, Saint Peter!*" With me hanging up here hot and bothered painting and plastering, having to listen to her. Well today, a voice comes through the roof. *Saint Peter is listening!* it says. *O Saint Peter*, she says, *what should I do?* And the voice through the roof says, *Close your eyes and keep them closed and Saint Peter will take care of you!* Then I hear footsteps and somebody jumping off the roof. And I'm alone with her."

"That face," said Carolita. "That hair."

"What did you do, wretch?" said Saint Peter.

"I took care of her, what else?" said Little Buddy.

"That's him!" said Carolita. "I kept my eyes closed but that's him!"

"Villain!" said Saint Peter.

"Hang him!" said Manuel.

"You said you wouldn't!" said Little Buddy. "You swore by the Lord!"

"That's true," said Jesus.

"We can whip him for lying, though," said the Sheriff. "What was that hogwash about a voice coming through the roof?"

"That was the truth," said Little Buddy. "Somebody was on the roof."

The Sheriff asked the Texans if they'd seen anybody on the Chapel roof at noon, and nobody had.

"Of course they didn't," said Saint Peter. "Because there wasn't anybody on the roof at noon!"

"Yes there was," said Jesus.

"Who?" said Saint Peter.

"I was on the roof at noon," said Jesus.

Everybody got very quiet.

"If this means," said the Sheriff, slowly, "that what I have got to do now is lynch the Lord Jesus by his dong, then I am turning in my badge."

"Lord!" said Saint Peter. "You!"

The Texans oohhed and aahhhed, shocked.

Jesus looked stern. He held up both hands. "Be seated," he said. He wasn't smiling now. The Texans sat in the pews. Jesus went up into the pulpit. He looked down upon them.

They shivered then, a little. Behind Jesus, sunlight came streaming through the newly scrubbed windows of colored glass. All that light made Jesus look radiant with power and majesty. He was suddenly not just a stranger in town. He was Jesus the Lord of Heaven and Earth, and everyone before him was filled with awe and fear.

"Manuel," he said. Manuel stood up.

"At the time for hunting, your dog is out peeing," said Jesus the Lord of Heaven and Earth.

Manuel sat down. "Carolita," said the Lord. Carolita stood up.

"A naked woman should not wring out her clothes," he said.

Carolita sat down. "Little Buddy," said the Lord. Little Buddy stood up.

"Don't jump too high under a low ceiling," said the Lord.

Little Buddy sat down. "Padre," said the Lord. The Padre stood up.

"What does an ass know about almonds?"

The Padre sat down.

"Fornicating Texans," said the Lord.

The Mayor, the Sheriff, the Blacksmith, the Mayor's wife, and every other Texan in the Chapel stood up.

"The horse who falls in love with his grass," said Jesus, "dies of hunger. Kill the snake, but don't break your stick."

The Texans sat down.

"Saint Peter," said the Lord.

Saint Peter stood up.

"Your frog caught a cold."

Jesus came down from the pulpit. He went to Manuel and Carolita. He put his hands on their shoulders.

"The world judges the deed," he said. "The baby judges the heart. You will have a little boy. Name him Pedro."

Then the Lord turned to everyone around him, and he said, "Those who have ears to hear, let them hear."

Jesus was smiling. The Texans began to smile, too. They looked around, and saw how restful the Chapel was now, with all the painting and plastering and hard work. What a fine place to come to, when life got too hard. They suddenly realized how much they had missed it.

The Sheriff started coiling up the hangman's rope. "How did this get started?" he said, like a man waking up.

"Saint Peter's Texas Claim," said the Blacksmith.

"You can forget that," said Saint Peter. "My week is up. I was only trying to cure you of carnal confusion."

"Yes, we know," said the Mayor. "How come you did that in the first place?"

"Because the Padre told me you were so corrupt you wouldn't go to Chapel any more."

"We didn't go to Chapel any more because the place was falling apart, and the Padre was always drunk."

"Yes," said Saint Peter. "He was overwhelmed by your carnal confusion."

Nobody could be sure exactly which came first.

"It's my fault," said the Padre. "What does an ass know about almonds?"

The Texans liked the sound of that, and congratulated the Padre on facing his defects like a man.

"Will you go to Chapel now?" said Saint Peter.

The Texans said they would, if Saint Peter and the Padre wouldn't worry too much about their carnal confusion. Saint Peter and the Padre agreed to that.

"Everything's all right, then," said Saint Peter, relieved.

"Not everything," said Jesus.

He stepped aside, and Saint Peter saw, standing behind him, his two loved ones he was always forgetting, and had forgotten again.

Perpetua and Petronella stood there, glaring at him. Petronella wasn't pretty at all any more. She was a crabby, mean, unhappy girl, even if she was an angel.

"Lord," said Saint Peter. "Why did you bring them here?"

"They aren't happy in heaven," said Jesus. "They say you're gone all the time."

"With you," said Saint Peter.

"I know," said Jesus.

"Well, explain it to them!" said Saint Peter, sharply. With all he had just been through, he lost his temper at the Lord. He blushed, seeing what he had done, but then felt another pang, just as deep.

His wife and lame daughter were looking at him with sullen reproach. Petronella was so miserable.

Saint Peter took a long, hard look at Jesus, and at his wife and child.

And he thought about his cottage by the lake, and how for years all he'd ever wanted was a good catch of fish, and the happiness of his family. He found Jesus instead. And here it was, centuries later, in Texas. His daughter still couldn't walk, not even as an angel in heaven.

It was time for a show-down, Texas style.

"Lord," said Saint Peter, firmly. "I never asked you before. But I will now. How could you tell me to follow you, and watch you cure people, and in your name cure them myself, and then never let me cure my own child?"

Jesus looked at the little family. It was so well-meaning and inept. It was earnest and indignant. It was everything helpless. Saint Peter's hair was all gone. Perpetua was all haggard and pale. Petronella was a bitter cripple.

Jesus laughed at them.

"The truth is," said Jesus, to Saint Peter. "I couldn't resist you."

But nobody else was laughing. Saint Peter looked very hurt. The Texans were upset. Perpetua was furious.

"What an awful thing to say," said Perpetua.

The Texans all nodded.

Petronella groaned.

"I was afraid you'd leave me," said Jesus.

"Leave you?" said Saint Peter.

"I was selfish," said Jesus. "I won't deny it. If you cured your child, you'd have stayed home. Who would have made me laugh?"

Now everybody was shocked.

"Sorry," said Jesus. "But that's the truth."

Saint Peter felt terrible. He would never have believed that of the Lord Jesus.

But Perpetua did.

"Well, Lord," she said. "I *am* angry! If Petronella could have walked, she could have married. She might have had a decent life. Now look at her."

"A two thousand year old virgin," said Petronella, bitterly.

"What can I do about it now?" said Jesus.

"Nothing," said Saint Peter, bluntly.

"Blessed be the name of the Lord," said Perpetua.

Petronella tried not to cry.

Now while this was going on, Little Buddy let his scaffold down from the ceiling. He waited until they all stopped talking. It was plain enough that nobody, not even Jesus this time, knew what to do.

Little Buddy cleared his throat, squared his shoulders and spoke right out, to Petronella.

"Pardon me," he said. "You have trouble getting married?"

"I sure do," said Petronella. "Nobody wants me."

"Nobody wants me, either," said Little Buddy. "Do you have a good disposition?"

"When I'm not chasing my father," said Petronella. "Yes, I do."

"Then I'll marry you," said Little Buddy. "If you'll have me."

"I'll have you," said Petronella. "But I'm an angel. I can't walk."

"That's all right," said Little Buddy. "I'll marry an angel. I've never had anybody, either."

"Except Carolita, you wretch," said Saint Peter.

"Now, Saint Peter," said the Mayor.

Jesus was smiling.

"Never mind about heaven," he said. "You can marry right here, and live in Texas."

"Can you do that?" said Perpetua.

"I can," said Jesus.

"Grandchildren?" said Perpetua.

"Lots," said Little Buddy. "To call you Granny."

"You want her to stay with you?" said Jesus.

"Yep," said Little Buddy.

"You sure?" said Jesus.

"I like Grandmas," said Little Buddy.

"Done," said Jesus. He turned to Saint Peter. "If that's all right with you," he said, politely.

"I don't know," said Saint Peter. "She's delicate."

"Not if she's been around for two thousand years," said the Sheriff.

"She's yours," said Saint Peter.

"Oh!" said Petronella.

"Thank you, sir," said Little Buddy.

"What's the matter?" said Perpetua.

"It's my legs," said Petronella. "They itch!"

She began to scratch them.

Little Buddy took her in his arms and kissed her.

"Oh!" said Petronella. Her left foot jumped. Her left crutch fell away.

"Hold on to me," said Little Buddy. "I won't let you fall."

And he kissed her again.

Petronella's right foot jumped.

"Oh!" she said again.

Her right crutch fell away.

"Kiss me back," said Little Buddy.

Petronella threw her arms around Little Buddy and kissed him like a grown-up woman.

"There," said Jesus, to Perpetua.

"There," said Perpetua, to Jesus.

And while Petronella kissed Little Buddy, the Mayor picked up her fallen crutches, and set them aside. Manuel opened a box and took out an accordion, while Carolita rattled two tambourines. The blacksmith turned around with a bass fiddle in his hands, and there the Sheriff was, holding a shiny violin and a horsehair bow.

They all grinned at Petronella and Little Buddy.

"Little Lady," said the Mayor. "What those feet want to do now is dance."

"Dance?" said Saint Peter.

"Dance," said Jesus.

"Whoo-pee!" shouted the Mayor, and *Whoo-pee!* shouted

the Texans. It was all right with Jesus, so they danced right there in the Chapel, and slowly Petronella began to dance, too.

She started out slowly, holding on tight to Little Buddy, but as the Texans clapped and stomped, as Little Buddy supported her, she began to trust her legs and moved faster.

Saint Peter watched her, tears in his eyes.

> *This is my vow:*
> *She will stand*
> *She will walk*
> *She will dance,*
> *Somehow!*

Now, at last, there she was dancing, all these centuries later.

Petronella swung herself about, legs pumping, graceful and gay.

"She's beautiful," said Saint Peter.

"That's right," said Jesus.

"And it was you wrote my name in that book."

"Right again."

"I'll get you for that."

"We'll see."

The dance went on, with the Lord and Saint Peter clapping, nodding, and tapping their feet, but inching a little closer to each other until they were standing there shoulder to shoulder.

Jesus whispered to Saint Peter.

"Coming with me?" he said.

Saint Peter smiled.

"Always," he said.

Over their heads, their halos appeared. They both began to rise, up, up, right up toward the Chapel ceiling, which now began to glow like fire.

"Oh, Poppa!" cried Petronella, dancing. "Goodbye!"
She waved to him.

"Goodbye, Lord!" cried the Texans, waving. "Goodbye, Saint Peter!"

Jesus and Saint Peter shouted down how much they had enjoyed it, left everyone dancing, and rose up from Texas to heaven above.

Epilogue

From the Gospel According to John

O righteous father, the world hath not known thee, but I have
known thee, and these have known that thou hast sent me.
And I have declared unto them thy name, and will declare it,
that the love wherewith thou hast loved me, may be in them,
and I in them.

Design by David Bullen
Typeset in 10pt Janson
at Dharma Press
Printed on acid-free paper